TVSK◐IVORIES

The phrase "it's a classic" is much abused. Still there may be some appeal in the slant of the cap Overlook sets in publishing a list of books the editors at Overlook feel have continuing value, books usually dropped by other publishers because of "the realities of the marketplace." Overlook's Tusk Ivories aim to give these books a new life, recognizing that tastes, even in the area of so-called classics, are often time-bound and variable. The wheel comes around. Tusk Ivories begin with the hope that modest printings together with caring booksellers and reviewers will reestablish the books' presence and engender new interest.

As, almost certainly, American publishing has not been generous in offering readers books from the rest of the world, for the most part, Tusk Ivories will more than just a little represent fiction from European, Asian, and Latin American sources, but there will be of course some "lost" books from our own shores, too, books we think deserve new recognition and, with it, readers.

Castle Gripsholm

Kurt Tucholsky

Translated from the German and with an introduction by
Michael Hofmann

Published by The Overlook Press

This Tusk Ivories edition first published in the United States in 2004 by
The Overlook Press, Peter Mayer Publishers, Inc.
Woodstock & New York

WOODSTOCK:
One Overlook Drive
Woodstock, NY 12498
www.overlookpress.com
[for individual orders, bulk and special sales, contact our Woodstock office]

NEW YORK:
141 Wooster Street
New York, NY 10012

Library of Congress Cataloging-in-Publication Data

Tucholsky, Kurt, 1890-1935.
Castle Gripsholm.
Translation of: Schloss Gripsholm.
I. Title
PT2642.U4S313 1988   833'.912   87-5766

Manufactured in The United States
ISBN 1-58567-558-X
1 3 5 7 9 8 6 4 2

Or we can blow our trumpets
And go blaring through the land;
But we'd rather walk in days of spring,
When primrose blossoms and thrushes sing,
Quietly thinking beside the stream.

THEODOR STORM

Christmas 2012

„Wir lagen auf der Wiese
und baumelten mit der
Seele."

Introduction

For twenty-five years, from 1907 to 1932, Kurt Tucholsky wrote polemical articles, feuilletons, theatre- and book-reviews, travel sketches, poems and cabaret songs. Then, for the last three years of his life, he was an ex-writer who expressed himself in his diaries and letters, but no longer in print. This deathly silence was part of his complete repudiation of Germany after the Nazi take-over. To have gone on writing – to have inveighed impotently against the coming to pass of what he had worked all his life to prevent – would have been to concede a defeat too bitter to contemplate. Erich Kästner described Tucholsky as 'a short, fat Berliner who tried, with his typewriter to avert the coming catastrophe.' The means proved insufficient.

Kurt Tucholsky was born in Berlin in 1890, the son of a prosperous Jewish businessman. Some of his childhood was spent on the blustery Baltic coast, for which he developed a lasting affection, and in whose landscape, people and language (all of them 'platt', 'low' or 'flat') *Castle Gripsholm* is a declaration of faith. In 1907, while still a law-student, he published *Rheinsberg: A Picture Book for Lovers*, a holiday story, a brief escape from the city into nature and love, a bitter-sweet not-quite-idyll of the sort he later developed in *Castle Gripsholm*. He took a doctorate in law – many of his fiercest attacks were reserved for the Weimar legal system, with its class justice and vicious political bias – and after the War, where he fought on the Eastern Front, he resumed his career as a writer and journalist. Working mostly for the weekly, *Die Schaubühne*, later *Die Weltbühne*, he soon found himself contributing under four pseudonyms as well as – decreasingly – under his own name. (A first selection of his pieces was accordingly called *Mit 5 PS, 5 HP*.) This 'blithe schizophrenia' is an extraordinary procedure that illuminates his nature as a man and a writer: firstly, it had a strongly practical side:

> 'it was useful to have a fivefold existence – because who in Germany will credit a political writer with humour? a satirist with seriousness? a whimsical fellow with knowledge of the penal code or a chronicler of cities with comic verse? A sense of humour loses you credence.'

Then, it was playful: the deployment of his five 'homunculi' as 'the five fingers of one hand' – although they had a fair degree of independence from one another, and sometimes fell out and conducted arguments among themselves! Lastly, it provided cover for Tucholsky himself, who, as he says near the beginning of *Castle Gripsholm*, disliked divulgence and confession in literature, and – appearances often to the contrary – kept his personal sphere intact. In the same way as his use of pseudonyms, Tucholsky's work combines practical value, discretion and playfulness.

In 1923, during the worst of the inflation, he gave up the profession of writing for a year and went to work in a bank. His experience of office life produced probably his best-known creation, Herr Wendriner, a version of the 'common man' of the 1920s: a Berlin Jew, a self-seeking survivor figure, rascally businessman and the hero of many sketches and monologues. The year after, he returned to writing, but left Germany for Paris, 'to take a rest from' his fatherland and gain a little distance from developments there: governmental weakness and deceit, militarism and exploitation, partisan justice, right wing paramilitary groups and political assassinations. From then on, he was only in Germany on occasional visits. Based mostly in Paris, he wrote and travelled.

In 1929 he moved to Sweden and in that year one of his most celebrated volumes, the satirically entitled *Deutschland, Deutschland über alles*, appeared, his texts to photos and montages by John Heartfield. Its tone is perhaps more despairingly aggressive than that of earlier writings, but the range remains typical: there is a long and closely argued attack on German justice; the caption 'Member of the Reichstag' over the picture of a cockatoo; some glorious monologues – a midwife enraged at being compared to a corkscrew; a circular proposing the leasing of civil servants to private groups, to provide official dignity and a few 'star turns'; ironic praise (from a rabid nationalist speaker) for the German army in the War, its 'painless style of close combat' and 'humane barrages'. There is a grisly picture of two duellists after a 'Studentenmensur', their faces streaming blood from what would turn into the 'scars of honour' they had received from one another. Above it is a poem entitled, with appalling accuracy, 'German judges of 1940'.

Tucholsky had always looked to the future, but what he saw there now made him incline to resignation and despair. His considerable popularity was not matched by any degree of actual political effectiveness: he doubted whether his work had got rid of a single official, or just one of those wicked, tortured and torturing 'Anstaltsweiber' ('institution-women' – like Frau Adriani) whom he particularly loathed. 'Are the sadists going? Are the bureaucrats being thrown out? It makes me depressed.' His writing now condensed itself into 'Schnipsel', 'snippets', that were either aggressive or troubled and pessimistic in character, though, somehow, they hadn't lost their wit:

'Germany is an anatomical curiosity: it writes with its left hand, but acts with its right.'

Another 'Schnipsel' describes man as 'a vertebrate with an immortal soul, and also a fatherland to make sure he doesn't get above himself'. Tucholsky's did, certainly. Just before Christmas in 1935, ill and unproductive and alone, 'broken by his fatherland', he took an overdose of morphia. He was buried in the churchyard at Mariefred, which he had described in *Castle Gripsholm*. 'If I had to die now,' he wrote, just before the event, 'I would say, "Was that all?" And: "I didn't really understand it." And: "It was a bit noisy."'

Castle Gripsholm was published in 1931. It is Tucholsky's only novel, his longest single piece of work of any kind. As a critic, he had a very high regard for the form, and so, despite his modesty in not claiming the tag for himself, tribute should be paid to the skill of this one (which has sold three-quarters of a million copies). More than anything else, it is a beautifully plausible version of what it pretends to be: 'a summer story' – the plainest and clearest and liveliest of first-person writing – full of fresh air, sunshine, trees, companionableness and friendly bickering – sweet oblivion. But, in the light of its author's other preoccupations, commitments and achievements, and of the date itself – two years later he would be stripped of his citizenship and his books would be burned – can this withdrawal, this holiday, this compliance with his 'publisher's' wishes, can it be real?

It is real, though the reality is wishful. That the sales of his books really did matter more than what he was trying to achieve in writing them. That it would be possible to turn away from politics, and to forget what was happening, in some serene privacy. That the struggle in Germany and for Germany could take place on some manageably small and symbolic level, like the struggle for Ada. That his privacy would indeed be serene . . . *Castle Gripsholm* is a book by a man who was never a father himself, and in whose life there were many women, but no one durable and fulfilling relationship. Tucholsky was not a visitor to the area of Mariefred and Gripsholm, he was living there, and he would die there and be buried there. The train that leaves Berlin at the beginning was one he had been on seven years before; a return to Germany and a resumption of his work there must have seemed at best problematic, and, more likely, out of the question. There is real sadness, and a real sense of farewell and ending in the last pages. No wonder perhaps that he leaves us with a drinking toast that is more an agnostic prayer in deadly times, out of sight of Sweden, and with his beloved German coastline never to re-appear.

In keeping with the 'blithe schizophrenia' with which he managed his four pseudonyms, Tucholsky's personal circumstances have been muted, dissembled and changed in a brave and resourceful way. Nothing could be further removed from the spirit of this book than self-pity, resignation and gloom. It has serious depths, but they have been concealed where it is most difficult and distinguished to conceal them: on the surface. The subjects of Tucholsky's publicistic writings – love and friendship, creativity and language, freedom and authority, nationalities, justice and modern life – appear everywhere: in conversations and casual reflections. Only in the astonishing, black reverie on gladiators and ancient Rome with its meditation and how a society keeps its members quiet by offering them violent spectacles, is there anything like a formal digression.

As well as finding the tone of *Castle Gripsholm* extraordinarily free and fresh, the reader may see a surprising modernity in the externals of a book written over fifty years ago. This comes in part from the abundance in it of those institutions that have more and more given texture to modern life: the office and the holiday, the customs and frontiers, the shop-window, the museum, the landlady and the boss. (The book is dedicated to a car licence-plate number.) In Stockholm, Tucholsky comments on the oppressiveness of modern cities, 'the occidental uniform, with American trimmings'. This awareness has something to do, I think, with Tucholsky's loneliness: a man with a home and loved ones would perhaps be more protected from the dominance of such neutral institutions, less painfully aware of their awful pervasiveness.

Tucholsky's loneliness can be indirectly – and surprisingly – laid at the door of Frau Adriani, one of his 'Anstaltsweiber', from a long string of authoritarian female figures in his work. The first of these occurred in 1914, in an article on the actress Rosa Bertens, playing a role from Strindberg:

'She sat in an upholstered chair, gripping both the arm-rests. Was she still in command? She had been in command for fifteen, twenty years, maybe longer, and they had been bitter years . . . This was her kingdom, and the view of the distant horizon was obstructed. She ruled here, ruled by all available means . . . There was the family table with the cosy lamp. A flight in the sunshine? You try flying when the lead weights of women drag you to the ground. Down! Down! Down! . . .'

What shows in these lines is of course not misogyny, but hatred of a home presided over by a dominant mother-figure, such as he himself had grown up in from the age of fifteen, when his father had died. As much as Rosa Bertens, the above portrait, as he told his second wife, was of his mother. So also is that of Frau Adriani, and it is she − with her taunts of 'Why don't you get married?' − who is at the root of the instability and impermanence of his marriages and other relationships. Tucholsky was far too good a student of Freud (who, with Strindberg and Hamsun, was one of his gods; he kept a photograph of him in his study) not to be aware of the implications of a poor relationship with his mother. By chance, this aspect too now looks modern: very few adjustments have to be made when one reads about the Princess and her 'Peter'. There is in their relationship hope and affection and sex and companionship, but nothing necessarily, unconditionally, formally binding. Will and inclination hold them together. They are not an entity, but two individuals, equal and independent, now adult, now childish, sometimes worried but never solemn. Their future (together) is uncertain. All the more reason, then, for them to make the most of their five weeks together, to talk and act and enjoy.

The particular difficulty in translating *Castle Gripsholm* has to do with what is perhaps Tucholsky's greatest gift as a writer: his ear for speech. In a word itself untranslatable, he calls himself 'ein Ohrenmensch', literally 'an ear-person'. It is the North German dialect, the 'Plattdeutsch' in the book that is the problem. Thomas Mann's translator, H. T. Lowe-Porter says frankly that 'dialect cannot be translated, it can only be got round by a sort of trickery which is usually unconvincing'. I have used little trickery. It seems to me that Tucholsky's Platt is so integral to the book, so firmly and repeatedly and deliberately described and celebrated that to search for a 'corresponding' dialect in English (then constantly referred to as 'Platt') would be mistaken. The very specificity of it would make it distracting, paradoxical, absurd. Tucholsky himself, in a review of a translation of *Lady Chatterley's Lover*, protested at having Mellors speaking in a 'Bavarian mountain dialect' that was quite incompatible with his explicit vocabulary. Similarly, what English dialect has recourse to French, to an antique genitive, or to some of Tucholsky's more carefully 'planted' idioms? I decided to aim for an understanding of the meaning of the German – difficult enough for a Saxon like myself, and someone whose sympathies tend to be with the taciturn Arnold anyway! – and to catch the Princess by the spirit, pace and tone of her speech, its qualities of parody and irreverence. I think it is still possible to 'hear' the book, even if not with its original genial locality. For help in understanding individual phrases, I owe thanks to my family, and rather more to Ebba Beer, Kay Hoff and Hans Werner Richter, who have the good fortune to be 'Plattdeutsch'. I am conscious of having rather dwelt in my Introduction on the darker hinterland of the book, but I am confident that its sunniness needs no introducing – only the reader's appreciation, and a little awe.

Michael Hofmann
April 1985
London

Chapter One

1

Ernst Rowohlt Publishers
Berlin W50
Passauer Strasse 8/9   8 June

Dear Herr Tucholsky,
    Many thanks for your letter of June 2. We have made a note
of your request. For the time being, though, another matter.
    As you know, we have been publishing mainly political books
recently. Quite enough of your time and energy has gone on
them. Now I think it's time we did something for *belles lettres*
again. Don't you have anything in that line? What would you say
to a short love story? Give it some thought. I'll keep the price
down, and print ten thousand copies to start with. Wherever I
go, my bookseller friends tell me how popular this kind of book
is. So how about it?
    We still have 46 Reichsmarks in royalties for you – where
would you like them sent?
            Best wishes,
            Yours
            [*enormous flourish*] Ernst Rowohlt

                                                    10 June
Dear Herr Rowohlt,
    Thank you for your letter of the 8th.
    A love story, . . . but, my dear master, how could I possibly?
Love in the present climate? Are *you* in love? Is anyone in love
these days?
    I'd rather write a little summer story.

It's not a straightforward business. You know I don't like bothering the public with my personal life, so that can be ruled out. Besides, there isn't a woman I don't betray with my typewriter, which makes my life thoroughly unromantic. And am I supposed to dream up this story? Only businessmen have any imagination – when they can't pay their bills. They can be *very* imaginative. The likes of us . . .

Unless I give people the stuff their fantasies are made of ('The Countess gathered up the folds of her silver gown, did not so much as look at the Count, and fell headlong down the castle steps'), all that's left is the problem of marriage as indoor gymnastics, 'the human angle' and all that stuff we so despise. And where is it to come from, unless you steal it from Villon?

While we're on the subject of poetry . . . how is it that in paragraph 9 of our contract you stipulate that 15% of all copies have no royalties payable on them? I know you'd never send out that many review copies! So that's why your authors are worked to the bone. No wonder you're drinking champagne on velvet cushions, while we lot sip weak beer on wooden benches. But that's the way it goes.

I always knew I was a credit to you. But being 46 Marks in credit that really *is* thrilling news. Please send it to the old address as usual. And by the way, I'm going on holiday next week.

> Best wishes,
> Yours,
> Tucholsky

Ernst Rowohlt Publishers
Berlin W50
Passauer Strasse 8/9   12 June

Dear Herr Tucholsky,

Thank you very much for your letter of the 10th inst.

As for the 15% of copies without royalties, they are – and this is the honest truth – my only way of making any money. My dear Tucholsky, if you could see our accounts, you would know things are not easy for a poor publisher. Without that 15%, I couldn't exist; I would simply starve. And you wouldn't want that.

You should think about that summer story idea of yours. As well as politics and current affairs, people want something they can give to their girlfriends. You can't imagine how big the demand is. I was thinking of a little novella, not too long, say 20,000 words, tender, paperback, gently ironic, and with a full-colour cover. You can make the contents as candid as you like and as a concession, I might even be prepared to go down to 14% without royalties.

What do you think of our new season's catalogue?

I wish you an enjoyable holiday, and am,

with all best wishes,

Yours

[*enormous flourish*] Ernst Rowohlt

15 June

Dear Herr Rowohlt,

Gulbransson has sketched you to the life in the new catalogue: 'quietly thinking beside the stream' – and reeling in the fat fish! The bait of 14% of copies without royalties isn't tasty enough: 12% would be more tempting. Just think about that for a bit, and give your hard publisher's heart a little nudge. I can't guarantee inspiration at 14% – the Muse starts at 12%

As I write this, I've already got one foot on the train. I'm leaving in an hour, for Sweden. I shan't do any work on this holiday; I just want to look at trees and have a proper rest for a change.

We can think about our project again when I get back. But, in the meantime, let me send you my best regards and wish you a good summer! And don't forget: 12%!

Best wishes,

Your faithful Tucholsky.

Signed – sealed – stamped. It was exactly ten past eight. The train from Berlin to Copenhagen was leaving at twenty past nine. We were off to collect the Princess.

17

She had a deep contralto voice; her name was Lydia.

Karlchen and Jakopp referred to every woman that any of us was involved with as 'the Princess', in order to honour whoever was her princely consort. So for the moment she was the Princess. But no other woman would ever be accorded the title again.

She wasn't a real princess at all.

In fact, she was something which contains every nuance you can possibly imagine: she was a secretary. She was the secretary of a monstrously fat boss; I had seen him once and found him horrible, and between him and Lydia . . . but no! That only happens in novels. Between him and Lydia there was a peculiar relationship: affection, nervous sufferance and trust on the one side; and affection, antipathy and suffering nerves on the other. She was his secretary. He affected the title 'Generalkonsul', but actually he dealt in soap. There were always packages of it lying about the office, which at least gave the fat man some excuse for his greasy hands.

In a fit of noble magnanimity, the Generalkonsul had allowed her five weeks off; he was going to Abbazia. He had left the night before – may he rest easy in his *wagon-lit*! His brother-in-law was in the office, and there was a replacement for Lydia. But what did I care about his soap? I cared about Lydia.

There she was in front of her house, with her suitcases.

'Hello!'

'Well, look who it isn't!' or words to that effect, said the Princess, to the utter astonishment of the taxi-driver, who clearly thought she was speaking Manchurian. But it was Missingsch.

Missingsch is what comes out when a Platt German from the North wants to speak proper High German. It slithers about on the carefully wax-polished stairs of German grammar, before falling flat on its face in its beloved Platt. Lydia came from Rostock, and she knew the idiom to perfection. There's nothing rustic about it – it's much more subtle. The proper German in it sounds like scorn and caricature, as though a peasant had gone out to plough his fields in a top hat and tails. And then Platt has all the humour of the North Germans: their good-natured debunking when someone comes on a bit strong, their lively sense of fun when they recognise pretentiousness – and they do recognise it, quite infallibly. Lydia could talk like that when the occasion arose. And here was such as occasion.

'I can't get over it, you haven't overslept!' she said, and, firmly and unhurriedly, set about helping me and the driver. We loaded up.

'Here, take the dachshund!' The dachshund was a fat handbag, elongated to the point of whimsy. How punctual she was! There was a hint of powder on the side of her nose. We drove off.

'Frau Kremser advised me,' Lydia began, 'to take my fur and plenty of warm coats – because there isn't any summer in Sweden, Frau Kremser said. It's always winter there. I hope it's not true!' Frau Kremser was housekeeper to the Princess, chambermaid, charlady and Keeper of the Great Seal. Her attitude to me, even after all this time, was still one of quiet and implacable suspicion – the woman had sound instincts. 'Tell me . . . is it really that cold up there?'

'It's funny, isn't it,' I said. 'When people think about Sweden, they think: Swedish punch, awfully cold, Ivar Kreuger, matchboxes, awfully cold, blonde women and awfully cold. It's not that cold at all.'

'Well, how cold is it, then?'

'Women are so pedantic,' I said.

'All except you!' said Lydia.

'I'm not a woman.'

'But you're pedantic!'

'Now excuse me,' I said, 'but there is a logical flaw here. It must be determined whether, *pro primo* . . .'

'Give Lydia a kiss!' the lady said.

I did so, while the driver wobbled his head about, because he could see us reflected in his windscreen. The cab stopped where all the better class of stories begin: at the station.

3

It turned out that porter no. 47 came from Warnemünde, so there was no end of exuberant chatter between him and Lydia,

until, worried about the time, I interrupted the idyllic reminisc-
ences of the two compatriots.

'Is the porter coming with us, then? Perhaps you could
continue your conversation on the train . . .'

'Don't get so steamed up, silly!' said the Princess. The porter
agreed.

'There's plenty of time yet,' he said.

Overruled, I shut up, and the two started an animated discus-
sion as to whether Karl Düsig was still living by 'the River' – you
know, Düsig – Naah! the old rascal! Yes, my goodness, he was
still living there! And had just produced another baby: the man
was seventy-eight years old, and as I stood there at the luggage
registration office, I felt quite extraordinarily envious of him. It
was his sixteenth. But now there were only eight minutes till the
train was due to leave, and . . .

'Do you want the papers, Lydia?' No, she didn't. She had
brought something to read with her. Neither of us suffered from
that peculiar disease of finding yourself at a station and suddenly
buying a couple of pounds of newsprint, when you can be pretty
sure in advance it will be tripe.

And so we got the papers.

Alone in our compartment, we set off via Copenhagen to
Sweden. But for the moment, we were still in Brandenburg.

'How do you like the scenery, Peter?' asked the Princess.
Among other things, we had settled on the name Peter – God
only knows why.

The scenery? It was a bright, windy June day – quite cool, and
the landscape looked clean and tidy – it was waiting for summer
and saying, I am bare.

'Yes,' I said, 'the scenery . . .'

'Now, for my money, you really could say something a bit
more profound,' she said. 'For instance, this landscape is like
frozen poetry, or it reminds me of Fiume, only the flora there is
more Catholic – something like that.'

'I'm not Viennese,' I said.

'Thank God for that,' she said. And we travelled on.

The Princess slept. I was thinking quietly to myself.

The Princess often accused me of saying, 'It's so nice that

you're there!' to every woman I was in love with, and she meant every one. Which was an awful lie, because sometimes I would say or think, 'It's so nice that you're there . . . and not here!' But when it was Lydia who was sitting next to me like this, I would say it and mean it. Why?

Because. In the first place . . . I don't know. We knew only this: one of the profoundest German sayings is about two people who 'can't stand the smell of each other'. We could, and that, if it lasts, already counts for a lot. She was everything to me: mistress, comic opera, mother and friend. What I was to her I could never discover.

And then there was her deep voice. Once I woke her up in the middle of the night, and when she woke with a start, I said, 'Say something!'

'You idiot!' she said, and fell asleep smiling. But I had heard her voice, I had heard that wonderful contralto voice.

And thirdly there was her Missingsch. Some people think Platt German is ugly and don't like it, but I've always loved it; my father spoke it as correctly as if it had been High German – Platt, 'the more nearly perfect of the two sisters', as Klaus Groth called it. Platt German is a mixture of everything: rough and tender, funny and sincere, clear, sober and, above all, it can be beautifully drunk. The Princess turned it into High German as it suited her – in fact there are hundreds of different sorts of Missingsch, from Friesland to Hamburg and across to Pomerania; every village speaks it differently. Philologically, it's difficult to grasp, but you can grasp it with your heart. That's what the Princess spoke – but not all the time! That would have been intolerable. Only sometimes, for a change, when she happened to feel like it, did she speak Missingsch: she used it for things that really mattered to her, and then she spoke it with a strong Berlin colouring. But she still spoke Platt sometimes, or that halfway Platt, Missingsch.

I'll never forget the time when we were first getting to know each other. I was having tea with her, and cutting the discreetly ridiculous figure of a man courting – we do make right idiots of ourselves. I was making calf's eyes at her and talking literature; she smiled. I told jokes, and lit up all the department-store windows of my heart. We talked about love. It was like a fight in Bavaria – when they fight, they begin with talking about it.

When I had explained everything to her, and my knowledge was not inconsiderable – I was very proud of the *risqué* things I'd dared to say, and of how I'd managed to present it all so precisely and with such burning clarity, so that really the time had now come to say: 'Yes, well how about it?' – then the Princess gave me a long look and said,

'What a sophisticated young man!'

And that did it. It wasn't till much later that I recovered again, still laughing, with nothing to show for my erotic baptism. But love had something to show for itself.

The train stopped.

The Princess sat up and opened her eyes. 'Where are we?'

'It looks like Stolp or Stargard – something with "St" at any rate,' I replied.

'And what does it look like?' she inquired.

'It looks . . .' I said, and gazed out over the little brick houses and the gloomy station, 'it looks like the sort of place where sadistic non-commissioned officers are born. Shall we have lunch here?' The Princess immediately shut her eyes. 'Or we can eat in the dining-car, they've got one on the train.'

'No,' she said, 'in the dining-car, the waiters are always infected by the speed of the train, and everything's such a rush. I've got a tummy that likes to take its time . . .'

'All right. By the way, what are you reading?'

'For the last two hours, I've been asleep, sitting on a fashionable novel. It's the only part of the body you can read it with.' She closed her eyes, then opened them again. 'Look at that . . . that woman! Isn't she misogynist!'

'Isn't she what?'

'Mysogynist . . . doesn't that mean stunted? No, I mixed it up with pygmies; they are those people who live up trees, aren't they?' After this performance, she dropped off again, and we travelled for a long, long time. As far as Warnemünde.

There was 'the River'. That's what they called the Warne here. Or didn't it have another name . . . Peene, Swine, Dievenow? It didn't say. For the sake of simplicity, Karlchen, Jakopp and I had decided to endow every town with a river of the corresponding name: Gleiwitz on the Gleiwe, Bitterfeld on the Bitter, and so on. There was a group of almost identical little houses down by the River, with the wind blowing round them, and looking so cosy. The masts of sailboats pierced the grey air, and loaded barges wallowed in the still water.

'Look, here's Warnemünde!'

'Now, I reckon I know a whole lot more about it than you do. Good Lord! That's the River, that's where I grew up, so to speak! Karl Düsig lives there, and old Wiesendörpsch, and that nice little house, that's where Kröger the decorator lives, such a nice man, there isn't a nicer man in the whole world. And that's Senator Egger's house, "Three Limes". And look – that old house with the pretty baroque gables – that one's haunted!'

'In Platt?' I asked.

'You're a cynic, aren't you! Do you suppose the Warnemünde ghosts go around with High German accents? No, there has to be propriety and order, even in the fourth dimension . . .! And . . .' Crash! The train gave a jolt. We fell on top of one another. She went on, and told me about every single house on the River, as far as you could see.

'There – that's the house where old Frau Brüshaber lived, she used to get terribly upset when I got a better report-card than her grandchildren; they were such creeps . . . she said if old Wiedow, the headmaster, had crawled up her ass, then she'd shit him straight into the Baltic! And this house used to belong to old Laufmüller. Haven't you read about him in your history-books? He was always at odds with the powers-that-be, which at the time meant District President von der Decken, Ludwig von der Decken. To annoy him, Laufmüller bought this mangy old dog and called him "Ludwig", and whenever von der Decken appeared, Laufmüller, with a broad grin on his face, would call his dog, "Heel, Ludwig, heel!" The District President used to get livid. What with all that going on, we didn't have a revolution here in 1918. Huh.'

'And is Herr Müller still alive?' I asked.

'Lord, no, he's been dead for ages. He wanted to be buried at the roadside, with his head directly underneath the road.'

'What for?'

'Well . . . so that he could go on looking up the girls' skirts as long as possible . . . Here's the customs!'

The customs. A man entered the compartment and politely enquired whether we . . . and we said no, we hadn't. And then he went away again.

'Can you see the point of that?' asked Lydia.

'I can't,' I said, 'it's just a game and a religion, the cult of the fatherland, which happens to be a blind spot of mine. I mean, look – this business with fatherlands and so on, they can only play that game for as long as they have enemies and frontiers. Otherwise, you'd never know where one stopped and the other began. You couldn't have that now, could you . . .?' The Princess opined that you couldn't. We were rolled onto the ferry.

We came to a standstill in a narrow iron tunnel, inside the steamer. With a judder, the carriage was secured.

'I'd like to know . . .' the Princess said, 'what makes a ship float. They weigh such a lot: why don't they sink? You're an educated bloke!'

'It's er . . . the air trapped in the bulkheads . . . you see . . . the specific gravity of water . . . well, really it's the displacement . . .'

'Love,' said the Princess, 'when someone uses that many technical terms, something's wrong. So you don't really know. It's a shame you're so awfully ignorant, Peter. But then I suppose you can't have everything.'

Up on deck we wandered the length of the ship, and from port to starboard. The engines were churning away very quietly. We pulled out of Warnemünde, and imperceptibly drew away from land. Past the end of the jetty we could see the coast.

There was Germany. You could just see a flat, wooded strip of coastline with houses and hotels, dwindling and receding, and the beach . . . Was that a very slight, faint, almost unnoticeable lurch? Let's hope not. I looked at the Princess. She sensed immediately what I was getting at.

'If you puked, laddie,' she said, 'that would really be a sooksay foo!'

'A what?'

'That's French.' She was getting very tetchy. 'Now he doesn't even understand French, when he's spent five years in Paris, learning about *Culture* . . . Tell me, what did you actually do all that time? I can imagine! Running around with the little French tarts, eh! Such a rake! What are they like, then? Come on, you can tell Lydia. We'll go up and down on deck, and if you feel sick, you can just lean over the railing, the way they do in books. Right!'

I told her that Frenchwomen were very sensible creatures, given to capriciousness, but always planning their caprices well in advance. Mostly they kept to one man apiece, a husband, or of course, a boyfriend – and perhaps a lover thrown in for the sake of respectability. And if they were unfaithful, they would be wildly cautious about it. But almost every other woman had a job. Though they didn't have the vote, they ran the country, not on their backs, but with their common sense. They were calculating darlings, with sensible hearts which sometimes ran away with them, but always brought them back. I didn't quite understand them.

'They sound just like women,' said Lydia.

The ferry wasn't quite rolling – it was only threatening to. I was threatening something, too, but the Princess ordered me into the dining-room. There they all were, sitting and eating. I didn't feel at all well when I saw that. They eat a lot of fatty foods in Denmark, and this was a Danish ferry. The assembled company were tucking into smoked eel and herring: herring fillets, marinaded herring, something they called *sild*, freshly caught herring and plain unvarnished herring. On dry land, each one more delicious than the last. To wash it all down, they were drinking that gorgeous schnaps for which all Scandinavians deserve to go to Heaven. The Princess deigned to eat. I watched, awestruck: she could hold her food.

'Won't you have anything?' she asked between two herrings. I looked at the two herrings, the two herrings looked at me, and none of us said anything. I only revived once the ferry had docked. The Princess gently stroked my knee and said respectfully, 'My little pirate!' I felt thoroughly ashamed.

We chugged through Lolland, which is as flat as a pancake, and we flicked through our newspapers. Then we played the book-game: each of us in turn would read out a sentence from his or her book. The sentences fitted together quite beautifully. The Princess turned the pages, and I gazed at her hands . . . she had such dependable hands. For a while she stood in the corridor, staring out of the window. Then she went off, and I couldn't see her any more. I reached for her bag, which retained the warmth of her hands. I stroked it. They ferried us across another stretch of sea, and then we chugged some more. At last, we reached Copenhagen.

'If we take a room over the courtyard at the rear,' I said in the hotel, 'then we'll get cooking smells, and the drunken Spanish composer will probably still be around from last time, composing ten hours a day on the piano. But if we take a room at the front, where the town hall clock strikes every quarter hour, we'll be reminded of time passing.'

'Couldn't we take somewhere in the middle . . .'

So we took a room overlooking the town hall square, the clock struck, and it was all marvellous.

Lydia picked at her food, and watched me admiringly. 'You do gobble . . .' she said agreeably. 'I've seen people who eat a lot, and people who eat quickly . . . but so much and so fast!'

'Pure envy,' I muttered, and turned to the radishes. It wasn't a gastronomic supper, but it was a very nutritious one.

As the clock struck, she turned over to sleep and I heard her say softly, as though talking to herself. 'You're on a ship now. There's a really heavy swell . . . a cup of luke-warm machine-oil . . .'

I had to get up and drink plenty of soda water.

4

Copenhagen.

'Shall I show you the sea-food restaurant where Ludendorff always used to eat, when he was still a war hero?'

'Yes, show me . . . no, let's go to the Lange Linie instead!' We looked at everything: the Tivoli Gardens, the beautiful town hall and the Thorwaldsen Museum, where everything looked as though it was made of plaster.

'Lydia!' I called, 'Lydia! I almost forgot. We absolutely have to visit the Polysandrion!'

'The . . . what?'

'The Polysandrion! You've got to see it. Come along.' It was a long walk, because the little museum was right outside the city.

'What is it?' asked the Princess.

'You'll see,' I said. 'It's where a couple of Balts built a house for themselves. One of them, Polysander von Kuckers zu Tiesenhausen, imagines he can paint. But he can't.'

'And we're going all this way just to see that?'

'No, not exactly. He can't paint, but he does – and he always paints the same thing, his adolescent fantasies: young boys and butterflies.'

'What's that supposed to mean?' asked the Princess.

'Ask him, he'll be there. And if he isn't, then his friend will tell the whole story. Because it has to be told. It's wonderful.'

'Is it at least improper?'

'Would I be taking you if it were, my raven-haired beauty?'

There stood the little villa – it was unattractive, and it didn't fit in here at all, either; you might have expected to find it somewhere in the south, in Tuscany or somewhere. We went inside.

The Princess' eyes grew round as saucers, and I beheld the Polysandrion for the second time.

Here a dream had become reality – may God protect us from the like! The good Polysander had covered about forty square kilometres of expensive canvas with paint. There were the youths, standing and reclining, floating and dancing. It was always the same picture, always the same young men. Pale pink, blue and yellow; the youths in the foreground, the perspective at the back.

'Those butterflies!' exclaimed Lydia, and took my hand.

'Shh!' I said. 'Not so loud! The cleaning woman is following us round. She'll report everything back to the artist, and we don't want to hurt him.' But really, those butterflies. They fluttered in the painted air, they had landed on the plump shoulders of the young men, and if until now we had thought that butterflies liked to settle on flowers, this was shown not to

27

be the case. These butterflies much preferred to perch on the young men's bottoms. It was all highly lyrical.

'Now I ask you . . .' said the Princess.

'Be quiet!' I said. 'His friend!'

The painter's friend appeared, quite an old, pleasant-looking man. He was very respectably dressed, but he had the air of despising the standard grey clothes of our grey century. And his suit got its own back by making him look like an emeritus ephebe. He murmured an introduction, and began explaining. In front of us was the picture of a young man who stood very upright with sword and butterfly, his right hand raised in salute. In the most beautiful, lilting Baltic tones, with all the r's rolled, the friend said, 'What you have before you is an entirrely spirritualised verrsion of militarrism.' I turned away – quite appalled. We saw dancing lads, in sailor-suits with floppy collars, and over their heads hung a little lamp with tassels – the kind you have in corridors. It was a sort of furnished version of the Elysian Fields. A whole Paradise had blossomed here, little bits of which so many of the painter's bosom friends carried around in their souls. Whether it was through being unjustly persecuted, or whatever it was, when they dreamed, they dreamed in soft sky blue, the pinkest shade of blue, so to speak. And they indulged in an awful lot of it. On one wall was a photograph of the artist in his Italian phase, dressed only in sandals and a Zulu-type spear. So paunches were all the rage in Capri.

'It takes your breath away!' said the Princess, once we were outside. 'They aren't all like that . . . are they?'

'No, you shouldn't blame the species for that. That house is just a plush sofa stuck in the 1890s; they're not all like that by any means. That man could just as well have peopled his chocolate-box paintings with little elves and gnómes . . . But imagine what a whole museum would be like, full of those fantasies come true – exquisite!'

'But it's so . . . anaemic!' said the Princess. 'Well, it takes all sorts! Let's drink a schnaps to that!' And we did.

The city streets: the animal wild-pack that belongs to the King, with its tame deer running wild and letting you pat their necks when they're in the mood; and those tall old trees . . .

Departure.

'What about the language problem?' asked the Princess when we were sitting in the train to Helsingör. 'You've been there before. Is your Swedish good?'

'I get by like this,' I said. 'First I speak German, and if they don't understand that, English, and if they don't understand that, Platt, and if that doesn't work either, then I stick an "as" ending onto German words, and I find they understand that quite well.' This was all we needed. She thought it absolutely wonderful, and immediately incorporated it into her linguistic paraphernalia.

'So it's Sweden next. What do you think will happenas to us now in Sweden?'

'Whatever happens on a holiday . . . You, I hope.'

'You know,' said the Princess, 'I'm not really on holiday at all yet. I'm sitting next to you in this compartment; but I've still got the office droning away in my head, and . . . Christ!'

'What is it?'

'I forgot to phone Tichauer!'

'Who's Tichauer?'

'Tichauer is the director of the N.G.S.W. – the North German Soap Works. My boss said I was to cancel him, because he was going on holiday . . . and the conference is on Tuesday . . . Oh blast!'

'So what do we do?'

'We'd best send him a telegram before we get on the ferry at Helsingör. Bloody hell! Oh, Poppa, why does Berlin always follow you around like that? It takes at least a fortnight to be rid of it, and just when you've managed to forget all about it, it's time to go back. What a wonderful profession!

'Profession . . . I always thought of it as more of an occupation.'

'You're only an author, but still you're right. Distract me. Stand on the seats and put on a show. Sing something – what did I take you along for?' Only calm and patience could help here . . .

'Look over there, those hens on the water!' I said.

'Hens? What sort of hens?'

'Visible hens. Jakopp the naturalist distinguishes between two types of hen: the visible hen, which you can only see, and the edible hen, which you can eat too. These are visible hens. How d'you like the country here?'

'A bit bleak, to tell the truth. If I didn't know we were still in Denmark and just about to cross over into Sweden.'

She had put her finger on it. Nothing distracts people from their real perceptions more than place-names, heavy with ancient longings and crammed with a multitude of associations. Then, when they finally reach the place, it's just a shadow of what they'd hoped it would be. But who would admit it openly?

Helsingör. We sent the wire to Tichauer and boarded the small ferry. Down below, in the ship's restaurant, were three Austrians. They were obviously aristocrats: one of them had that very languid voice. He narrowed his eyes in a peculiar way, like someone paying a bill with a cigar in his mouth, and I heard him mutter, 'Sound fellow – rather mediocre . . .' I'm not in favour of the Anschluss.

We stood on deck, by the railing, breathing the clear air and looking at both shorelines: the Danish coast behind us, and the Swedish coast approaching. I watched the Princess out of the corner of my eye. Sometimes she was like a complete stranger, but I kept falling in love with this stranger, and having to win her all over again. The distance between a man and a woman! But then how lovely, to dive into a woman like diving into the sea, without thinking . . . Many of them wear glasses, as it were; they have forgotten what it is to be a woman in the real sense. They just have that thin layer of charm left. Damn it! I suppose we ask a bit much of them: intelligent conversation, logic, good looks and a certain degree of fidelity – and yet there is still that irrepressible longing to be gobbled up like a beefsteak by the woman with jaws crunching . . .

'Do you have any Swedish currency?' asked the Princess dreamily.

'Yes, I have some Kroner,' I said. 'It's a lot of money, and we'll have to be careful how we spend it.'

'Skinflint,' said the Princess.

We had a joint travelling fund, which it had taken us six months to work out. We were in Sweden.

Customs again. Swedish German is different from Danish German. With the Danes, it's a faint exhalation, which sounds light as a feather. The consonants emerge half a yard in front of the mouth, and dissolve in the air like birdsong. With the Swedes it comes from further back in the throat, and with a wonderful lilt . . . I showed off horribly with my ten words of Swedish, but no one understood them. They probably thought I was some particularly complicated type of foreigner. We had a light lunch.

'The bouillon,' said the Princess, 'looks like water in half-mourning!'

'That's just what it tastes like too.' We went on to Stockholm. She slept again.

To watch someone sleeping is to feel superior to them – it's probably something left over from prehistoric times, perhaps it's the dormant thought: he can't hurt me, but I can hurt him. At least she didn't look foolish; her breathing was quiet and firm, and her mouth stayed shut. That's how she'll look when she's dead. Then her head will be resting on a board. Whenever I think of death, I see rough, unplaned boards, with little splinters. She'll be lying there, the colour of candle-wax, but there will be something awe-inspiring about her. Once, when we were talking about death, she said, 'We all have to die – you sooner, me later.' Her thinking could be so masculine. The rest, thank God, was all woman.

She awoke. 'Where are we?'

'In Rüdesheim on the Rüde.' And then she did one of the things for which I loved her most, something she did in special psychological moments: she put her tongue between her teeth, and quickly withdrew it again, producing a blind whiplash of spray. She got a kiss for that – on this journey, we always seemed to have a compartment to ourselves – and immediately she used a newly acquired Danish oath: 'May the Devil embroider you in baby pink!' And then we started to sing.

In Kokenhusen
sings a nightingale
In Duna by the sea.
And the nightingale
singing sweetly
drops a present in my hand

Just when we were singing at the tops of our voices, the first houses of the city came into view. Points clicked, the train rattled over a low bridge and came to a halt. Come on! Suitcases. Porter. A cab. Hotel. Hello. Stockholm.

5

'What shall we do now?' I asked, when we'd washed. All we could see of Stockholm from our hotel window was four chimneys against a blue sky.

'I think,' the Princess said, 'we should first get an interpreter – your Swedish is excellent, quite excellent . . . but it must be ancient Swedish, and the people here are so uneducated. So we should take an interpreter out into the countryside and find a very cheap little cottage, and we'll stay there very quietly. I don't want to travel another kilometre ever again.'

We took a walk through Stockholm.

They have a lovely town hall and attractive new houses. A city with water is always beautiful. Doves were cooing in a square and the harbour smelled of tar, but not quite strongly enough. The women in the streets were gorgeous . . . of a quite mesmerising blondness. And you could only get schnaps at certain times, which acted as a powerful spur on us to drink some – it was clear and pure, and didn't do you any harm so long as you remained sober. As soon as you'd drunk it, the waiter would whisk the glasses away, as though he had been party to some crime. In a shop-window on the Vasagatan was a Swedish translation of the latest hit song from Berlin.

Well, and is that all you saw of Stockholm? Eh? And the national character? Ah, friends! How monotonous our cities have become! Go to Melbourne and spend a long time talking and arguing with the businessmen. Then, if you really want to get to know them, marry their daughters or do a deal with them or, better still, share an inheritance with them. You have to sound out what is below the surface . . . you won't be able to see it at a glance. What is there to see? The same tram-bells ring everywhere, policemen raise their white-gloved hands, everywhere the same colourful posters for shaving-soap or women's stockings. The world has put on an occidental uniform, with American trimmings. It's no longer possible just to go out and see the world; you have to live with it, or against it.

The interpreter! The Princess' idea was a good one, and we went to the office of a tourist-agency. Yes, they had an interpreter. Maybe. Definitely. Yes.

They are deliberate in Sweden – very deliberate. There are two types of Swede: the agreeable Swede – a quiet, friendly man – and the disagreeable Swede. He is extremely proud and so obtuse he doesn't notice how pig-headed he is. We were dealing with one of the helpful sort. An interpreter, yes, they had one, and they would send him along to our hotel the next morning. Then we went to eat.

The Princess knew about food, and in Sweden they ate well, so long as you stuck to cold hors d'oeuvres – to Smörgåsbord. Unsurpassable. Their cooking was average, and they didn't have a clue about red wine, which rather distressed me. The Princess didn't drink red wine much. Instead – and she was the only woman I've ever met who did – she liked whisky. Most women say it tastes just like a dentist's mouthwash, but if it's good whisky, it tastes of smoke.

The next morning the interpreter arrived.

A fat man appeared, a mountain of a man. This was Bengtsson. He could speak Spanish and very good English, as well as German. Or rather: I listened once . . . I listened twice . . . he must have learned his German in America, because he had the brightest, loveliest and funniest American accent. He spoke German like a circus clown, but he was what Berliners call 'proper'. He understood immediately what we wanted, and immersed himself in maps, timetables and brochures. By the afternoon we were on our way.

33

We went to Dalarne. We toured the countryside around Stockholm, and rattled along dusty country roads to the remotest villages. We saw sullen fir-trees, stupid pines and majestic old deciduous trees under a blue summer sky scattered with white, cotton-wool clouds; but we didn't find what we were looking for. And what was that? We wanted a very small, very quiet little cottage, secluded, comfortable, peaceful, with a little garden . . . that was what we had dreamed of. Perhaps no such thing existed.

Our fat man was absolutely tireless. While we drove around looking, we asked him about his job. Yes, he guided foreigners around Sweden. Did he really know all the things he told them about? By no means – but he had lived in America for a long time, and he knew his Americans. Figures! He gave them plenty of figures: dates and dimensions and prices and figures, figures, figures . . . Didn't matter if they were wrong. His German became more fluent with every day he spent with us, but it also became more American.

'Three weeks back,' he said, when we had just returned from another unsuccessful expedition and were having supper, 'three weeks back, there was this American family in Stockholm. I said to them, it takes just one visit to America, and you realise that the whole of the rest of the world is like an Amurrican callany. Yup. After that, the people rilly took to me in a big way. Bottoms up!'

Bottoms up? We were in Sweden, he should be saying 'Skål!' Skål is the same as 'shawl'. Seeing that the Princess was a poor foreigner who didn't understand us Swedes properly, I said, 'Shawl to you!' and all three of us understood.

The fat man ordered himself another schnaps. He stared dreamily into his glass. 'In Göteborg lives a guy with a big cellar – he's got everything there, whisky, brandy and cognac, red and white wine and champagne. But, instead of drinking it, he's saving it all! I think that's rilly turrific!' With that, he knocked his own glass back.

By now the days were passing, and we had listened to endless conversations, and heard innumerable people saying what Swedes always say, at everry possible juncture, 'Yasso . . .' and 'Nedo', and all the other things people say when they have nothing to say. Our fat man had guided us to many beautiful places, through wonderful rich forests. 'Here are some fine-looking trees!' he would say. The Princess was beginning to jib a little.

'He's laughing all the way to the bank,' she said. 'My dear lovely Pops, we're no Rockefellers. Now put your foot down once and for all and tell him what we want!'

What now? Our fat man was walking ahead of us, pensive, but pretty well pleased with the world. He banged the pavement with his stick and was thinking hard; you could tell from his broad back how hard he was thinking. Then he growled because he had thought of something.

'We'll go to Mariefred,' he said. 'That's a little place . . . it's all right! We can go there tomorrow!'

The Princess shot me an ominous look. 'If we don't find anything there, Poppa, I'll stick you in a children's home, and go off and join my boss in Abbazia. That'll concentrate your mind!'

But the next day we did see something.

Mariefred is a tiny little place on the shores of Lake Maelar. The landscape was quiet and peaceful, with meadows and trees, fields and forests – but no one would have paid any attention to it, had it not been the site of one of the oldest castles in Sweden: Castle Gripsholm.

It was a radiantly clear day. The red bricks of the castle glowed, its round domes seemed to erupt into the blue sky. But the building was solid, weighty, seigneurial. Bengtsson waved the guide away, he would show us round himself. We went into the castle.

There were many fine paintings inside. They did nothing for me. I can't see. There are visual types and aural types; I can only hear. A variation of an eighth of a tone in a conversation will still be with me four years later, but a painting is just something colourful. I don't know anything about the architectural style of this castle – I only know that if I were to build one for myself, I would build it like that.

Herr Bengtsson explained the castle to us, the way he might have explained it to his Americans. He'd been consulting a bottle or two, and after every date he added, 'But I'm not quite sure about that,' so we looked it up in *Baedeker*. It was all wrong, all of it, and we were delighted. There was a dungeon, where Adolfus the Unshaven had been kept locked up for years by Gustavus the Constipated. The castle had very thick walls, and there was a round cage for prisoners, and a gruesome oubliette, or perhaps it was a well . . . Man has always tormented man, only today it takes different forms. But the best thing was the theatre. They had a little theatre in the castle – perhaps so that they wouldn't get bored during sieges. I sat down on one of the benches in the auditorium, and put on a pastoral comedy for myself, with love and duelling and sighing and refined tippling – and then the Princess became quite forceful. 'Now or never!' she said.

'Right – Herr Bengtsson!'

Like all good-natured men, our fat man was scared of women – he bent his soul as a traveller bends his back under a shower of rain. He made a big effort, and really threw himself into action. He was on the telephone for a long time and then disappeared.

After lunch, he returned in high spirits, his fat rippling with contentment. 'Come with me!' he said.

The castle had an annexe. If asked, Fatty would surely have replied, 'In the twenty-first century . . .' It was fairly new, long, smooth-fronted, handsome. We went in, and were met by a very friendly old lady. It turned out that there were two large rooms and another, smaller one to let in this castle-annexe. Right here in the castle? I looked disbelievingly at Herr Bengtsson. Here in the castle. And she would cook for us. But wouldn't we be disturbed by countless tourists coming here to take in the paintings and the torture-chamber? They only came on Sundays, and they never came round this way, they went over there . . .

We inspected the rooms. They were nice and big; there was old castle furniture in them, in a heavy, comfortable style. With my blind spot, I could see none of the details – but the style spoke to me, and it said yes.

One of the windows overlooked the lake, another a quiet little park. The Princess, with female practicality, was assessing the bathroom situation . . . and came back satisfied. The price was surprisingly low. 'Why is that?' I asked Fatty. Even when faced with good fortune, we tend to be suspicious. The lady of the castle did it out of friendship for him, because she knew him. And people didn't often come here for a longer stay. Mariefred was well known as a place for excursions; and such a reputation tended to stick to a place. So we took the rooms.

When we had taken them, I spoke those golden words, 'We should have . . .' and got a friendly smack from the Princess.

'You old moaner.' We celebrated the agreement with a big brandy for the three of us.

'Do you know her well, the lady of the castle?' I asked Herr Bengtsson. 'She's been so kind to us!'

'You know,' he replied thoughtfully, 'everyone knows the monkey, but – the monkey knows no one.' We had to agree with him there. Then Fatty said goodbye. The suitcases arrived and we unpacked. We re-arranged all the furniture until it was all back where it had been to begin with . . . the Princess took a trial bath, and I rejoiced at the way she crossed the room naked – like a real princess. No, not like a princess, like a woman who knows she has a beautiful body.

'Lydia,' I said, 'there was a Dutch girl in Paris, who had a tattoo on her thigh, over the place she wanted to be kissed on. Can I ask you . . .' She answered. And here begins section

6

We lay in a meadow, bathing our souls.

The sky was flecked with white; when you had been roasted by the sun for a while, a cloud would come along, a light wind would blow, and the temperature would drop a little. A dog trotted over the grass, a good way behind us.

'What kind is it?' I asked.

'A bull dachshund,' said the Princess. We let the wind blow over us some more, and said nothing. It's nice to have someone you can share a silence with.

'Damn,' she said suddenly, 'it's awful – but I'm not really here yet. God damn my job in Berlin. My head is still buzzing with the old boss and all that . . .'

'How is he now?' I asked idly.

'Well . . . same as ever . . . He's fat, curious, cowardly and mean. Apart from that, he's quite nice. Fat, that would be all right. I don't mind fat men.' I made a movement. 'Don't you start getting ideas . . . your little spare tire!'

'You probably think you're something special, just because your name is Lydia. Now let me tell you . . .'

When the conversation had calmed down again, she continued, 'All right then, fatso. But his curiosity . . . what he'd really like would be for me to give him some new bit of gossip from the trade every day. He's a spiritual voyeur. He doesn't himself participate in most things, but he wants to know exactly what everyone else is doing; how, who with and how much they earn – especially that! And what they live on . . . What? How does *he* earn his money? He does it by bare-faced cheek. Oh, Poppa, we could never do that! For four years I've had to watch how the Herr Generalkonsul manages, for instance, to avoid paying his bills on time . . . we couldn't behave like that, which is why we'll never be rich. You just wouldn't believe it! It doesn't matter who he's dealing with; he's so brazen, he'll twist a signed contract or he'll repudiate it altogether, then he'll suddenly forget what his excuse was . . . No, Cheri, you'd never be able to operate like that. You might want to, but you'll never do it!'

'Do people let him get away with it?'

'What else can they do? If you don't like it, he says, you can sue me! But it'll be the last time you ever get an order out of me! And he sticks to that quite rigidly. People know that – and in the end they give in. Just recently, the whole office was redecorated; you should have seen how he treated the workmen! But that's how you get to go to Abbazia, while the workmen walk across the Alexanderplatz. That's life.'

'And in what way is he mean?'

'That must be genetic – I think generations must have contributed to it. It can't be the work of just one man. If his best friend wanted to do him a favour, he would have to break his leg on my boss's birthday. I've never seen anything like it. He really looks for opportunities to rejoice at the misfortunes of other people . . . Maybe it's so that he can prove to himself how superior he is. Whenever he's being rude, he thinks he's very superior to you. That must be it. He's so unsure of himself . . .'

'It's often that way. Have you noticed how often rudeness can be attributed to uncertainty?'

'Yes . . . What a jolly place Berlin is! But what am I supposed to do? They say, A woman like you! Whenever I hear that! Marry some drip . . . You may laugh, Poppa, I can't bear that type. Well, their money. But it's not just the *wagon-lits* and the big cars, it's when they talk! And especially when they let themselves go a bit . . . Come on, let's go in, it's getting cold.'

It was early evening by the clock, but here it was still light. Even though Gripsholm wasn't that far north, the Arctic sun still shone and it was only dark for a few hours, and then not completely. We walked over the meadows and looked at the grass.

'Let's have supperas!' said the Princess in Swedish.

We ate, and very reverently I drank water with the meal. When you're in a foreign country, first of all you have to let the foreign water gurgle inside you, to get the flavour of the place. We sat and smoked. Now the holiday began, the real holiday.

The bedroom curtains were tightly drawn and pinned shut with needles. Men can only sleep in pitch darkness; the Princess saw this as a male characteristic. I read.

'Don't rustle the newspaper so angrily!' she said.

That night the Princess turned over and slept like a stone. She hardly breathed; I didn't hear her. I read.

Sometimes, in the grip of a nightmare, I would start up and cling to the Princess . . . ridiculous!

'Do you want to save me?' she would ask laughingly. It had happened two or three times – often I wouldn't even know.

'Last night you saved me again . . .' she would say the next morning. But it was the holidays now; I certainly wouldn't be saving her tonight. I put my hand on her as she slept. She sighed gently and shifted in bed. It's nice to be together. The skin doesn't get cold. Everything feels quiet and good. Your heart beats calmly. Good night, Princess.

Chapter Two

As well as I could, said the boy –
then they broke the stick over his back.

I

The girl stood by the window, thinking, When will this ever end?
It will never end. When will this ever end?

She had both arms propped on the windowsill, which wasn't
allowed – but for one instant, for one tiny, stolen instant, she
was alone. The others would be arriving any minute now; it was
your back that sensed them first of all, as it was nearest the door;
there would be an expectant tickling in your back. And when the
others arrive, that's it. Because then *she'll* be there too.

The little girl shuddered: it was like the slight, sudden movement of a dog shaking itself dry. She didn't even have to think
about the things that were oppressing her. She was surrounded
by sorrows, sitting on one lotus-leaf among many, with the
others all watching her – the girl in the middle. And she knew all
the lotus-leaves of her sorrows.

The other children – her nickname 'the child' – this children's
home in Sweden – her dead brother Will – and now the needle of
her fear shot up into the boiling red area: Frau Adriani, Frau
Adriani with the red hair – and behind her the saddest thing of
all, Mummy in Zurich. It was too much. She was nine years old –
it was too much for nine. And she cried the bitterest tears that a
child can cry: suppressed tears that no one can hear.

The patter and scrape of feet. Doors shutting and opening.
Not a word: a silent host was approaching. She was there too.
Oh God! Oh God!

The door opened majestically, as though of its own accord. In
the doorway stood the Director, 'the Limb of Satan': Frau
Adriani. Her nickname came from her own favourite term of
invective.

40

She wasn't very tall: a squat, thick-set figure, with reddish hair, greyish-green eyes and almost invisible eyebrows. She spoke rapidly and had a way of looking at people that did them no good at all . . .

'What are you doing here?' The child cringed. 'What are you up to?' She went up to the girl and gave her a cuff on the head – it wasn't a proper smack; it was a blow that didn't acknowledge that there was a head there: it dealt with whatever material was available. Which happened to be a head.

'I was . . . I . . . I'm er . . .'

'You're a limb of Satan!' said Frau Adriani. 'Mooning around up here, while there's a gym lesson downstairs! No supper for you. Join the rest!' The child crept off to join the others; proudly and with a show of contempt they made room for her.

Läggesta was a children's home, mainly for German children, and with a few from Denmark and Sweden. In this way, Frau Adriani made full use of her property on Lake Maelar. Two nieces helped her with the work: one, like an extension of her aunt, was as feared and hated as she was; the other was gentle but downtrodden and timid. She tried to intercede when she could, but she was rarely successful. When the older woman had one of her days, her two nieces were nowhere to be seen. She had forty children. She had no children. The forty had a hard time of it. The woman took trouble over the children, but she was hard and she beat them. Did she enjoy beating? She liked power. Every child that left the home before time was, in her eyes, a traitor – to what, she couldn't have said – and every one that joined it was a welcome addition to the domain she ruled over. Even if many of the children complained and were taken away, there were many orphans, and new girls kept arriving.

Giving orders . . . it wasn't easy to do that otherwise. Because when the Swedes give way, they do it with a gracious bow, and because they have agreed. They only obey when, at a certain point, they see that it's necessary, useful or honourable to do so . . . otherwise, someone wanting to give orders has few opportunities in this country. They wouldn't understand him; they would laugh at him and do as they pleased.

Frau Adriani made frequent changes in her staff, bringing new employees back from Germany, where she regularly went on visits. In winter, she sat up there almost deserted, only a few children left to her – like little Ada for example. Her husband . . . when Frau Adriani thought of her husband, it was like having to brush away a fly. That man . . . she didn't even shrug her shoulders any more. He sat in his room, putting his stamps in order. She earned the money. All winter she would wait for the summer – summer was her time. In summer she could boom down the long corridors of her villa, commanding and forbidding and decreeing, and everyone around her would be asking each other what sort of mood she was in, and they would tremble with fear. She relished that fear to her fingertips. To feel other people's wills under her own was . . . it was life itself to her.

'Everyone is to stay up here till the bell goes. No supper for anyone talking. Sonya! Your hair-ribbon!' One of the girls went scarlet, took out of her hair a ribbon that had come undone, and tied it again. It was so quiet – you could hear forty little girls breathing. With a glare from her grey-green eyes, Frau Adriani took in the scene, then went out. Behind her back, a two-sided whispering started up: there were those who wanted to talk, very quietly, and the others who tried to stop them by going 'Sshh!' The child stood all by herself. Little girls can be very cruel. As no one else had been punished that day, the majority had tacitly decided that the child was to be ignored. The child was called 'the child' because once, in answer to Adriani's question 'What are you?' she had replied 'A child'. No one paid her any attention now.

When will this ever end? thought the child. It will never end. And then her tears flowed; she was crying just because she was crying.

2

The trees rustled outside the window, and they rustled me out of a dream. Even as I woke up, I had already forgotten what it was. I turned over on the pillows; they were still heavy with my dream. Forgetting . . . why had I woken up?

There was a knock.

'The post! Poppa, it's the post! Answer the door!' The Princess, who the instant before had been asleep, was awake – there was no in-between.

I went. Between the bed and the door, I thought about these morning-moments between a man and a woman when love can be pretty dead. Critical moments, but if they pass, everything is all right. From the first croak of 'What time is it . . .?' to the 'Huuargh – there, I'm getting up now!' the little bedside clock ticks away a lot of time. The day has woken up, the night is asleep, the subterranean hemisphere is asleep . . . a pity, with the majority of women at least . . . I was at the door. A hand was pushing letters into the letter-box.

The Princess had half-sat up in bed, and in her excitement pillows were going everywhere. 'My letters! Those are my letters! Give me them, you thief! Do I have to . . .' She got her letter. It was from her replacement at work, and the news was that there was no news. The business with Tichauer had been sorted out all right. In the little inventory book they had reached G. I was most relieved to hear it. The worries of these people! What worries did they have? Their own, remarkably.

'Go and heat up some water!' said the Princess. 'You need a shave. You're in no state to kiss anyone looking like that. What was your letter about?' I grinned and hid it behind my back. The Princess wrestled with the pillows. 'Probably one of your women . . . one of those old Excellencies you adore so much . . . Show it here. Show it to me, I said!' I didn't.

'I won't show it to you!' I said. 'I'll read you the beginning. I swear I'll read it as it's written, word for word. I swear. Then you can see it.' A pillow fell out of bed, exhausted and battered to death.

'Who's it from?'

'It's from my Aunt Emmy. We had a quarrel. Now she wants me to do something for her. That's why she's writing. It says:

"My dear boy, Just before my cremation, I take up my quill . . ."'

'I don't believe you!' cried the Princess. 'That's . . . give it here! That's rilly great, as Bengtsson would say. Now go and shave, and stop holding everybody up with your cremated aunts!'

Later we went out into the countryside.

Castle Gripsholm radiated into the sky; it was calm and solid and watchful. The lake rippled slightly and played against the shore. The boat to Stockholm had already gone; you could just make out a faint trace of smoke behind the trees. We headed in the opposite direction from the lake.

'The lady at the castle,' said the Princess, 'speaks a sort of private German. She just asked me if we were warm enough at night – she was sure I was a little ice-cake . . .'

'That's lovely,' I said. 'You're never sure with northerners whether they're translating literally from their own language, or whether they're unconsciously making up new phrases. In Copenhagen I knew a woman who said, in her furious bass voice, "This Copenhagen isn't a capital city – it's a capital hole!" Do you think she made that up?'

'You know so many people, Poppa,' said the Princess. 'It must be nice . . .'

'No, I don't know nearly as many people as I used to. What's the point?'

'I'll tell you something, my boy,' said the Princess, who was really smitten with her Platt German today. 'When you meet someone that you can't quite make out, you should just ask yourself: will he give me love or money? If it's neither, then let him go and don't waste your time with him! All the same, is that any reason to tread in that cowpat!'

'Damnation!'

'You shouldn't swear like that, Peter!' the Princess said unctuously. 'It's not right. Let's lie down for a while on that grass over there!'

We lay down . . .

The woods rustled. The wind blew through the tree-tops, and a delicate scent rose from the ground, fresh and sour, of moss and pine resin.

'What would Arnold have said if he were here?' I asked cautiously. Arnold was her ex; when the Princess was in a very good mood, one might risk reminding her of him. She was in a good mood now.

'He wouldn't have said anything,' she answered. 'He didn't

have anything to say anyway, but I only realised that much later.'

'Not very quick then?'

'There's more sense in my wastepaper basket than there is in his head! He didn't talk much. At first I thought his silences were terribly meaningful, but he just wasn't much of a talker. You get them sometimes.'

A footfall on the soft moss; a little boy came stumbling along the forest path, muttering something to himself. When he saw us, he stopped, looked up at the trees and started running.

'That could have been a case for the public prosecutor,' I said. 'With his ingenuity, he could have built up a whole case just from that. But the little boy was probably just reciting his tables, and felt embarrassed when he saw us . . .'

'No, it was like this,' said the Princess. She lay on her back and told her story to the clouds:

'A boy was sent to the shops one day for soap and salt. So he kept singing to himself, soap and salt . . . soap and salt . . . But he didn't watch where he was going, and he tripped over a string in a bean-field. Hell's bells! A string and beans! String and beans! he said – and he stuck with string and beans, and ended up buying them. Oh, Peter! Peter! What's life all about! Tell me quickly, what? I don't want to hear any more foul language . . . I know all the words anyway. What is it about? I want to know right now!'

I sucked the end of a bitter fir-twig. 'First of all,' I said, 'I saw how it was. And then I understood why it was like that – and then I appreciated why it couldn't be any other way. But I still want it to be different. It's a trial of strength. If you can remain true to yourself . . .'

In her deepest contralto voice she said, 'After all the times you've proved how true you are to me . . .'

'I wonder if it's possible to have a serious conversation with a woman. I don't think so. And they go and give the creatures a vote!'

'That's what my boss always says too. I wonder what he's up to now?'

'He's probably bored, but really pleased with himself to be in Abbazia. Your Generalkonsul . . .'

'Come on, Poppa, you've got your writer's pride too. You know, sometimes I think the man has made it after all. He wasn't born a Generalkonsul, with his soap and his safe and everything. He's always telling me what a comfortable life he's had – which means he hasn't. He probably had a lot of lean years before they let him get at the cream. And now he's licking his chops . . . What? Of course he's forgotten the lean times. They all do. Memory, my boy, memory . . . it's like an old barrel organ. Nowadays people have gramophones! If only you could find out what it's like when someone makes it to the top – someone like my boss . . . He's not married . . . but even if he was, his wife wouldn't be able to tell you either, she wouldn't have noticed anything. For her, success would be only natural, and people just don't want to know about a hard grind to the top, because that would be admitting that their own ancestors were running around without a visor. Promotion . . . they just say that when they don't want to give you a pay-rise.' Thus spoke the sage Princess Lydia, and concluded her speech with a magnificent –

The Princess began to hiccough.

She wanted me to lift her up but with a beautifully athletic bound she stood up by herself. Slowly we crept back through the forest. We stopped at every little glade and made speeches, each of us pretending to listen to the other, and to admire the forest, and really doing both. But, if we'd been asked, we'd have had to confess that in our hearts, although we weren't in Berlin anymore, we weren't yet in Sweden. But we were together.

We passed the first house in Mariefred. A gramophone was scratching away.

'It's come here to convalesce,' said the Princess in hushed tones. 'You can hear it – it's still quite hoarse. But the air here will do it the world of good.'

'Are you hungry, Lydia?'

'I'd like . . . Peter! Poppa! Oh, God! What's the genitive of Smörgas . . . I'd like some Smörgassens . . . Oh blast!' All this kept us occupied until we were sitting down at table, and the

Princess had gone through the declension of the Swedish hors d'oeuvre.

'What shall we do after lunch?'

'What a question! After lunch we're having a nap. Karlchen always says there's such a lot of fatigue trapped in one's day clothes . . . you have to take them off and have a proper rest. And you sleep. That restores your energy.'

'Tell me, is your friend Karlchen still polishing his chair at that Revenue Office in the Rhineland?'

I said he was.

'And what's special about him, then?'

'Now look,' I said to the Princess, 'he's quite exceptional in every way! But one couldn't tell him that because he would get so conceited, peacock feathers would sprout from his ears. He's a . . . well, Karlchen's just Karlchen!'

'That's no explanation. That's just like my Konsul when there's something he doesn't want to say. I'm going to bed, to get some sleepas.' I heard her singing to the tune of Tarara-boom-diay:

> And then the little horse
> suddenly turned about
> and with a flick of his tail
> he brushed away the flies –

The trees rustled in our sleep.

3

In the afternoon we stood in front of the castle – tourists were coming and going.

We walked around the castle garden; there was an ornate well in the middle and little oriel-windows jutted out from the walls. The castle had been renovated . . . a pity. But maybe the whole edifice would have fallen down otherwise. It was old enough.

A large tourer drove up.

A young man got out of it, then two ladies, one older, one younger, and finally a fat gentleman was scraped out of the back.

They spoke German, and stood round their car looking perplexed, as if they had just arrived from the moon. The fat man spoke loudly and rapidly to the driver, who fortunately didn't understand.

They bought tickets for the castle but the guide had already gone home, so they were left to do the pilgrimage on their own.

'Lydia . . .' I said. We set off after them.

'What's the plan?' Lydia asked, lowering her voice. She had understood what I was thinking.

'I'm not sure yet,' I said, 'I'll think of something . . . Come along!'

The tourists were standing in the Great Hall, looking up at the panelled ceiling. One of the ladies said, so loudly that it echoed, 'Not bad!'

'Obviously Swedish style!' observed the fat man. They muttered.

'Now if they were to ask whether this was all built . . . Quick!'

'Where to?'

'To the big well. We'll put on a performance for them there . . .'

We could hear them shuffling about and coughing – then we were out of earshot. We walked quietly and fast.

We came to the large round chamber with its wooden gallery. In the middle of the earthen floor was a circular wooden disc which was the entrance to the dungeons. We found a ladder. Lydia helped, and we dropped the ladder in. Hurray! It stood up! So the dungeon couldn't be very deep. I climbed down, pursued by looks of mock admiration from the Princess. 'Give my love to the bats!'

'Shurrup!' I said.

I went down – quite a long way . . . like an American film-comedian miming a fireman. That's what it looked like, but I didn't feel terribly amused. Where was I going? But I would do anything for a laugh. Only darkness and dust and the round beam of light from above . . . 'Some matches please! From your handbag!' The box came down and landed on my feet. I stooped and hit my head on the ladder – then I found it. A light . . . it was a large room. Rings had been set into one wall; evidently they

didn't correct their prisoners by easy stages, but all at once . . .
There was a further well-hole, too.

'Lydia?'

'Yes?'

'Pull the ladder up – can you manage? I'll help you. I'll lift it – har-rupp! There . . . have you got it?' The ladder was back up. 'Put it away!' I heard the Princess moving the ladder away. 'Put the cover back on, will you? And hide.' Now it was completely dark. Black.

It's strange, when you're not used to it. The moment you find yourself in complete darkness, it feels inhabited. No, you expect it to be inhabited; you're afraid of it, and so you long for some living presence. I cleared my throat gently, to show that I was still there, and had no hostile intentions . . . I groped in the darkness. There was a nail in the wall, I wanted to keep hold of that . . . Ah? There they were. You could hear their voices quite distinctly; the wooden disc was very thin.

'There's nothing here,' said a voice. 'Probably a well – for sieges and that sort of thing. Very interesting. Well, let's go on. Nothing here.'

There will be, you wait.

'Huuuuuuu!' I wailed.

There was deathly quiet above. The dragging footsteps stopped.

'What was that?' someone asked. 'Did you hear it?'

'Yes, I thought so too – probably just a noise.'

'Huuuuuuu-aa-huuuuuuu!' I howled again.

'For god's sake Adolf, perhaps an animal has been shut in there, a dog, come along!'

'Now really, I can't believe it! Is – erhem – is someone down there?'

I kept very quiet.

'An illusion,' pronounced a man's voice.

'Come on! It wasn't anything,' said the other man.

I thought of the lions at the zoo before feeding-time, and drawing a deep breath I began to roar,

'Huuuuuuu-brru-aa huuuuuuuuah!'

That was too much. One of the women shrieked, and then

49

there was the noise of people legging it, but one still managed to say: 'But it's quite . . . there must be an explanation . . . we'll ask at the gate . . . incredible . . . I mean it's . . .'

'Come along there! What do we have to go to all these castles for anyway . . .'

They were gone. I stood in my darkness, dead still.

'Lydia?' I whispered. No answer. Some dirt trickled down the wall. Hm . . . A sound? But everything here is wood and stone; there was no noise. I listened. My heart was pounding a little faster than I would have liked. Nothing. It's wrong to give people a fright, you see, it's wrong . . . 'Lydia!' Louder still, 'Halloo! Hey! You!' Nothing.

Thoughts flashed through my brain: it was just a joke. Served them right. Keep still, or you'll get your clothes dirty. You're scared. You're not scared. It's superstition. Lydia's just coming. What if she's fainted, or she's died suddenly, then no one will know you're down here. That only happens in films. Pathé did something like that once. It's cruel to lock people up in the dark. Once in the war, I saw someone released from a dark cell, the light made him giddy. Then he started crying. He hadn't come up to scratch as a soldier, so they locked him away, that's wrong. Give judges a taste of the sentences they dish out. But that won't work, because they'll know it's just a taste. Hence the folly of the death sentence, when no one knows what it's like. By now my heart was beating regularly, I was thinking, and letting my thoughts run on . . . The wooden cover moved; it was pushed aside. Light. Lydia. The ladder.

I climbed back up. The Princess was laughing her head off. 'How did you get into such a state? Come over here – you're going straight back to our rooms! God, what a sight!'

I was grey with dirt, festooned with spider's webs, my hands were streaked with black and the rest of me was equally filthy.

'What'd they say? What did you do? Oh boy, just take a look at your silly face in the mirror!'

I decided I'd rather not.

'What kept you, woman? Leaves me languishing in a dungeon! That's love for you!'

'I . . .' said the Princess, putting her mirror away again, 'I was looking for a loo, but there wasn't one. The old lords of the castle must have had chronic constipation!'

'Wrong,' I said donnishly. 'Incorrect and uninformed. Of course they had certain localities for that purpose, which led into the moat, but when they were being besieged, well, then . . .'

'It's high time you had a wash now. You pig!'

We strolled over to our rooms, past the greatly astonished landlady, who must have thought I'd been drinking. I emerged, brushed and washed and with a fresh collar. I had been severely scrutinised by the Princess who had sent me back three times; each time she found more dirt.

'Whom shall we annoy now?'

'You're going too far. Nothing but silly pranks in his head, and he wants to be a serious man!'

'I don't want to . . . Have to. Have to.' We went outside.

Some way off was a little pavilion, where the group from the car was sitting, drinking coffee. We strolled past chatting to each other. The younger of the two men got up and came over to us.

'You're from Germany . . .?'

'Yes,' we said.

'Well . . . would you like to join us at our table perhaps?'

The fat man got to his feet. 'Teichmann,' he said. 'Direktor Teichmann. My wife. My niece, Fräulein Papst. Herr Klarierer.'

Now I had to reply, because that's the custom of our country after all.

'Sengespeck,' I said, 'and my wife.' Whereupon we sat down and the Princess kicked my shins under the table. Coffee. Plates rattling. Cake.

'Very nice here – I take it you've come on an outing too?'

'Yes.'

'Charming. Very interesting.' Pause.

'Er . . . tell me . . . is the castle actually inhabited?' The Princess kicked me hard.

'No,' I said, 'I don't believe it is. No. Certainly not.'

'Ah . . . we thought perhaps . . .'

'Why do you ask?'

Significant looks were exchanged.

'We just thought . . . it seemed to us we heard someone talking in one of the rooms – but strange, more like a dog, really, or a wild animal . . .'

'No,' I said, 'I think I can assure you there are no animals living in the castle. Or almost none.' A pause.

'Anyway . . .' said Herr Direktor Teichmann and looked around, 'there's not much going on here! Don't you find?' We agreed nothing went on here. 'You know,' said the Direktor, 'if you really want to enjoy yourself, there's only Berlin. Or possibly Paris. But really only Berlin. It's in a class of its own. No?'

'Hm-' we murmured.

'And I don't think it's at all smart here either!' said Frau Direktor Teichmann.

'I imagined something completely different,' added Fräulein Papst. 'Where shall we go tonight in Stockholm?' asked Herr Klarierer. But Frau Direktor Teichmann didn't feel like going out; the episode in the castle had made her nervous. By now, the Princess had twisted a ring from my finger and opened one of my cuff-links, all under the table – and I thought that was enough. Who knows what else she might . . . So we took our leave, saying we were expected in the town.

'Are you going back to Stockholm later on?'

No, we were afraid we weren't.

We were still 'afraid not' when we were standing in the meadows again, and happy; happy that we didn't have to go to Stockholm, that we were in Sweden, that we were on holiday . . .

'What's that?' asked the Princess, who had eyes like a hawk. A thin row of little figures was coming through the meadows, on one of the narrow paths. 'What is it?'

They drew nearer.

They were children, little girls in pairs, all in a line, like a double-row of pearls. A bossy-looking person was leading them, glaring round all the time – none of them were talking. As they came closer to us, we stepped aside to let the procession pass. The leader threw us a glittering look. The children trotted on. We didn't speak as they filed past us. At the very end was a little girl on her own; she walked as though she were being pulled along, her eyes were stained with tears, she still sobbed occasionally as she walked, but she wasn't crying. Nor was her face puffy, as a crying child's sometimes is . . . instead, it looked as though it had been emptied of tears; there was a golden shimmer in her brownish hair. She looked at us as she might have looked at a tree, tired and indifferent. In a fit of exuberance and kindness, the Princess offered her a couple of harebells we had picked. The child quivered, then looked up, her lips moved; perhaps she wanted to say something, to thank her . . . but just then the woman at the front turned round and the little girl quickened her step and hurried after the troop. Dust and the sound of the children's marching feet. Then it was all over.

'Funny little girl,' said the Princess. 'What sort of children are they? Let's ask later. Peter, my son, do you get Northern Lights here? I'd so like to see some Northern Lights!'

'No,' I said. 'Yes, of course, but everything you want to see, my daughter, happens the month you're not there . . . Life's like that. But that comes in the next lesson. Northern Lights – yes . . .'

'I think they must be lovely. I saw them once as a child, in an encyclopaedia. That was a world of its own, too, that encyclopaedia, with its little leaves of tissue-paper. There they were, illustrated, the Northern Lights, very big and bright, they're meant to cover half the sky. I think I'd be terribly scared if I saw them. Just imagine, big coloured lights in the sky! What if they fell! And landed on your head! But I would love to see them just once . . .'

The pale-blue sky arched over our heads; at one point on the horizon it turned a deep dark-blue, and where the sun had gone down earlier, it glowed a rosy yellow, and shone and twinkled a little.

'Lydia', I said, 'shall we make our own Northern Lights?'

'Well . . .'

'Look,' I said, and pointed up at the sky, "you see, you see – there – there they are!"

We both looked fixedly up – we were holding hands, our pulses and our blood flowed from one to the other. Just then, I loved her more than ever before. And then we saw our Northern Lights.

'Yes,' said the Princess quietly, so as not to frighten them away.

53

'It's marvellous. Light-green – and there – pink! And spirals – and that, so high . . . Look, look!' Now she dared to speak louder, because the Northern Lights were up there like the real thing. 'That looks like a little sun!'

I said, 'And that, that's curdled milk and there, baby cirrus-clouds . . . blue . . . light-blue!'

'Look, and the horizon, I'm sure it just goes on and on – it's all silver grey. Oh Poppa, isn't it beautiful!'

We stood still and looked up. A wagon rattled past and made us start. The farmer, sitting on the driver's seat, waved to us and looked up himself to see what it was. We looked first at him, and then at the meadows, which were cold and grey. A little ashamed, we smiled. We looked back up at the sky. There was nothing there. It was smooth, blue and twilit. There was nothing.

'Peter . . .' said the Princess, 'Peter . . .'

4

'Could you tell us, Frau Andersson,' I said to the castle lady, who had just wished us good evening – I pronounced her name correctly, 'Andershon' – 'who were those children we saw earlier? Back . . . back in the meadows?'

'Ah yes, there are many children. They are farmers' boys who gather and play there . . .'

'No, no. They were little girls walking along in a very orderly line, like an institute or a school, something like that . . .'

'A school?' Frau Andersson thought for a while. 'Ah! They are Frau Adriani's children. From Läggesta.' And she pointed to the other side of the lake, where you could just see a large building in a clearing. 'That's a boarding school, a children's home. Yes.' She had an expression on her face such as I had never seen before. I grew curious. Now, it's conventional wisdom that it's better not to ask a direct question – because then you won't get the answer you're looking for.

'There must be a lot of children there . . . are there not?'

'Yes, a holy mess,' said Frau Andersson; you often had to guess at her meaning a little, as she probably translated everything directly from the Swedish. 'There are many children boarding there, but not many Swedish children. Praise God!'

'Why praise God, Frau Andersson?'

'Jaha,' she said and veered away like a hunted rabbit, 'there are not many Swedish children, ne-do!'

'That's a shame,' I said, thinking I was being awfully subtle. 'It must be very nice there . . .'

Frau Andersson was silent for a moment. Then, courageously, she took a little run-up. She lowered her voice.

'There is . . . it isn't a good woman who is there. But I don't want to speak evil . . . you understand. A German lady. But not a good lady. German people are so friendly – not true . . . Please don't mistake me!'

'You mean the headmistress of the boarding school?'

'Yes,' said Frau Andersson. 'The headmistress. The head-distress is a bad person. Everyone here thinks that. She's not to our taste. She's not good with the children.'

'Well,' I said, and looked at the trees, whose leaves trembled slightly as if they were shivering. 'Well – not a good lady then? What does she do wrong? Does she shout at the children?'

'I'll tell you,' said Frau Andersson, and she turned to the Princess, as if this was a matter exclusively for women, 'she is hard to the children. The headmistress . . . beats the children.'

The Princess gave a start. 'Doesn't anyone mind then?'

'Jaha . . .' said Frau Andersson. 'She doesn't beat them that hard. So the police can't say anything. She doesn't hit to make the children sick. But she is unfair, the children are afraid from her.' She pointed to a castle-like building on a hill behind Mariefred: 'I prefer to be there than with that woman.'

'What is that building?' I asked.

'That is a mental asylum,' said Frau Andersson.

'And so the mental patients are better off than those children?'

'Yes,' said Frau Andersson. 'But I want to see now whether dinner is ready . . . one minute.' And she went away hurriedly, as though she'd said too much.

We looked at one another. 'Funny, isn't it?'

'Yes, well, it happens,' I said. 'Probably some demon of a woman, applying the iron rod.'

'Peter, play me something on the piano till it's time for supper!'

We went into the music room of the castle, which the lady had said we could do, and I sat down in front of the little piano and played a few cheerful melodies. I stayed mostly on the black keys; they are easier to hit. I played:

> Sometimes I think of you,
> but it don't agree with me . . .
> because the next day I feel so tired –

and:

> Ah, the hedgehogs at eventide
> were off chasing mice,
> and I was hanging on your lips –

We sang old folk-songs and American songs, and then a riding-song which we had composed ourselves, and which was completely idiotic from beginning to end, and then supper was ready.

We had got hold of a bottle of whisky. It wasn't easy, because we didn't have a *Motbok*, the little booklet that entitles you to buy spirits in Sweden. But we had got the bottle. And it hadn't even been that expensive. Blonde and brunette . . . Black and White . . . here's to you . . .!

We sat at a wooden table in front of the house and looked over at the castle.

Every now and again, we took a sip of whisky.

The old church clock struck ten – ten o'clock. The air was still; not a leaf moved on the trees – all was peaceful. White nights. There was a feeling of rigidity, as if something was building up and nature was holding her breath. Light? It wasn't light. It just wasn't dark either. The branches loomed black; they were waiting. As if the skin had been stripped from everything: the night stood there shamelessly, without darkness, deprived of blackness. You wanted to conjure up the black cloak of night, and throw it over everything, so that nothing could be visible any more. The castle had lost its burning red, and looked a dull brown, then murky. The sky was grey. It was night, without being night.

'It should always be as quiet as this, Lydia – why is there so much noise in life?'

'Dear boy, you won't find silence any more these days – I know what you mean. No, it's been lost for all time . . .'

'Why doesn't it exist?' I went on. 'There's always some noise. Someone knocking, or music, or a dog barking, or someone tramping about in the flat above, windows rattling, the phone ringing – God should have given us earlids. We've been incorrectly designed.'

'Stop babbling,' said the Princess. 'Listen to the silence instead!'

It was so quiet, we could hear the soda singing in our glasses. Our drinks stood in front of us, a brownish colour; the alcohol was quietly entering my bloodstream. Whisky removes your cares. I can easily imagine someone destroying himself with it.

A bell rang in the distance, as though frightened out of its sleep, then everything was quiet again. Our house was a grey-white colour; all the lights were out. Silence arched over our heads like a giant bowl.

At that moment we were both quite alone, she on her female star, and me on my male planet. Not enemies . . . but far, far apart.

From the brown whisky three or four red ideas climbed into my blood . . . crude, indecent, squalid. They came, whooshed past, and then they were gone. My mind retraced the shape the feeling had sketched. You swine, I said to myself. There you are, you've got this wonderful woman . . . you're a dirty old man.

We're all animals underneath, said the swine. Don't fool yourself!

I won't have it, I said to the swine. You've caused me so much pain and unhappiness, so many bad hours . . . not to mention the fear I might have picked up some infection. Forget about those subterranean adventures! They're not even that wonderful – you just imagine they are!

Hehe! snorted the swine, so it's no fun? Now just imagine . . .

Quiet! I said. Quiet! I don't want to.

Oui, Oui, the swine said and wallowed shamelessly; just imagine there was . . .

I killed it. For the time being, I'd killed it – let's say I shut the sty. I could still hear it rumbling away crossly . . . then the glasses were singing again, very, very quietly, like the hum of a mosquito.

'Poppa,' said the Princess, 'do you think it would be all right to wear the blue suit I brought with me?'

I was back with her; we were sitting on the same planet again, rolling through the universe together. 'Yes,' I said. 'Do.'

'Is it suitable?'

'Of course. It's quiet and discreet, should be perfect.'

'You shouldn't smoke so much,' she intoned with her deep voice, 'or you'll be sick again, and who has to put up with the consequences? Me. Put your pipe away.'

As her son, I put the pipe away, because that's what my mother wanted. Quietly I laid my hand in hers.

5

The big house in Läggesta had been built by masons – who else. Craftsmen; quiet, thoughtful men, who look three times before they do anything. It's the same the world over. When it was finished, they plastered the walls, and some of the rooms were painted, many more were papered, all differently, and according to their instructions. Then they had gone away phlegmatically. The house was finished; it didn't matter what happened in it now. That wasn't their affair, they were only the builders. The courtroom where people are tortured was, to begin with, a rectangle of brick walls, smooth and whitewashed. A painter had stood on his ladder and whistled cheerfully as he painted a grey stripe right round the room, as he had been told to; as far as he was concerned, it was a piece of craftsmanship . . . and now, all at once, it was a courtroom. People build theatres for future scenes with complete detachment; they erect a stage and wings, they construct the whole theatre, and then others play their sad comedies there.

The child lay in bed, thinking.

Thinking . . . A long time ago, when she still had a father, she always used to play at 'thinking' with him. Her father had laughed so; he had a marvellous laugh.

'What are you doing?' the child would ask.

'I'm thinking,' her father would say.

'I want to think too.'

'Fine . . . you think too!' And he would earnestly pace up and down the room, with the child following him in an exact imitation of her father's posture, with her hands clasped gravely behind her back, and wrinkling her brow the way he did . . .

'What are you thinking?' her father would ask.

'I'm thinking – a lion!' the child replied. And her father would laugh . . .

Next to her, Inga breathed hard and tossed in bed. The child was suddenly back where she really was: in Sweden. In Läggesta. Mummy was in Switzerland, so far away . . . the child felt a flush of heat rising inside. She had written so many imploring letters, well, three, only three really – and then the Limb of Satan had found out that one of the maids had been secretly posting the letters. The maid was sacked, the child had her hair pulled, and now all letters to Switzerland were vetted. Perhaps it had to be like that. Perhaps her mother had no money to keep her at home, and it was cheaper up here. That was how her mother had explained it.

She was so alone here. Quite alone among the other thirty-nine girls, and she was afraid. Her life consisted of nothing but fear. Fear of the Limb of Satan and of the older girls, who would tell on her whenever they could, fear of the next day and of the day before, from which things might come to light. Fear of everything, everything. The child didn't sleep – her eyes made holes in the dark.

That her mother could have sent her here! They had been here once before, three or four years ago – and her brother Will had died. He was buried in the churchyard at Mariefred. The child could sometimes visit his grave, when the Limb of Satan let her or told her to. Usually she told her to. Then she would stand by the little grave, the fourteenth row on the right hand side, with the little headstone, where the letters still gleamed as new. But she had never cried there. She only cried sometimes at home for Will – fat little Will, who was younger than she was, and wilder at games and a good boy. Now and then Mummy had had to smack him, but it never hurt, and he laughed under his child's tears and would be a good little fellow again. As if he was made out of rubber. And then he became ill. Flu, people said, and four days later he was dead. The child still remembered the hospital smell. But all that hadn't happened here, it had happened in Taxinge-Näsby, a name she'd never forget. The sour smell, the 'Hush!' as everyone went around very quietly on tiptoe, and then he had died. The child had forgotten how. Will wasn't there any more.

Not her brother. Nor her mother. Father had gone away – where to? No one was there. The child was alone. She didn't think the word – it was much worse: she felt loneliness, as only children can feel it.

The little girls rustled in their beds. One was whispering in her sleep. It was her second summer up here. It would never be any different. Never. Why doesn't Mummy come here, the child thought. But she would have to take her away with her, because even Mummy was no match for Frau Adriani. No one was. Footsteps? What if she came now? Once Gertie had been ill; then Frau Adriani had come up five times in the night – five times to look after the little girl, and fought almost jealously with her illness. In the end she had conquered the fever. What if she came now? Silence – one of the eight beds creaked. That was Lisa Wedigen, she was always a restless sleeper. If only somebody – somebody – somebody . . . Tomorrow they were going swimming in the lake. The girls always splashed you, if only somebody –

Her hands felt carefully under the pillow, searched the bedding, moved all the blankets. Gone? No. They were still there.

Under the pillow, wilted and crushed, were the two harebells.

Chapter Three

Eggs is eggs, he said –
and grabbed the biggest

I

We bent over the letter and read it together:
Dear Chap,
   I still have a week's holiday owing to me this year, and I'd very
much like to spend it with you and your lady friend. I hear you're
in Sweden. Dear friend, would you like to put up your old
comrade-in-arms, who gave you a leg-up in the odd shell-hole or
two? I'll pay for my own transport; it hurts me to have to spend
money on myself; it's not my usual way of doing things, as you
know. Write and tell me, dear friend, how to get to you.
   Can I stay there? Are you staying there? Are there lots of girls?
Should I not come? Shall we get drunk on our first evening
together? Do you love me?
   I enclose a picture of my little girl. She's almost as beautiful as
her father.
   I'm looking forward very much to seeing you, and am your
good
   Karlchen.
   Underneath, in red ink, like a mark on a file, there was:
'*Straightaway! Yesterday, preferably! Indescribably urgent!*'
   'Well,' I said. 'That's Karlchen, then. Should he come?'
   The Princess looked tanned and refreshed. 'Yes,' she said, 'let
him come now. I've had a rest, and if he's leaving after a week
anyway? It's always nice to have a change.' I wrote accordingly.
   We were in the middle of our holidays.
   Swimming in the lake; lying naked on the shore, in a sheltered
spot; soaking up the sun, so that you rolled home at noon,
wonderfully dozy, and drunk on the light, the air and the water;
quiet; eating; drinking; sleeping; resting – holiday.

Then the day arrived.

'Shall we go and pick him up?'

'Yes, let's.'

It was a glorious day – perfect weather for laying eggs, as the Princess put it. We went to the station. It was a tiny station; really just a little house, but it took itself so terribly seriously as a station, that it had quite forgotten it was a house. There were two pairs of rails, as every station has to have, and there was the carriage puffing noisily. It wasn't a train as such, only a single carriage-cum-locomotive. It had put on a little smokestack, to give it some credibility. It pulled in. Hissed. Karlchen.

As always when we hadn't seen one another for a long time, his expression was equable, friendly, a little foolish, a sort of 'Ah . . . so there you are . . .' expression. He came up to us, the shadow of the imminent greeting already visible on his face, and carrying a tiny little suitcase. He was a tall fellow, and his slightly battered face looked 'youthful and alert', as he put it.

Hello – this is . . . meet . . . now shake hands . . . where's the rest of your luggage? When the preliminaries were over, I asked,

'Well, Karlchen, how was your trip?'

He had fluttered up to Stockholm, he said, in an aeroplane, arriving at noon . . .

'Was it nice?'

'Well . . .' said Karlchen, and bared his teeth in his habitual grimace, 'there was an old lady who didn't take to flying very well. Give me a cigarette, will you. Thanks. And they have these little bags . . . She had already used up two of them, and the third didn't reach her in time, so the man next to her will either have to buy himself a new suit, or have his old one cleaned. Unfortunately, I wasn't sitting next to her. The rest of the view was very nice. And how does Madam like it here?'

As Karlchen said 'Madam', which he didn't himself believe in, he stiffened and politely inclined his upper body; he accompanied this with a charming gesture, abruptly extending his forearm and then withdrawing it again with the elbow bent, as if he had wanted to inspect his cuff-links . . .

And how was Madam enjoying it?

'If *he* wasn't here,' Madam said, 'then I would be having a very restful time. But you know what he's like – always blathering on – never leaves you in peace . . .'

'Yes, he was always that way. How nice,' he said suddenly. 'I've left my umbrella on the train.' We went back to get it. Things don't disappear in Sweden. The two came to an immediate understanding – it's strange how, within the first few minutes people often determine the entire future course of their relationship. Here you could sense immediately that the two of them had hit it off: they took *Life*, and me in particular, less than seriously.

Karlchen was still exactly as he had been a year ago, two years ago, three years ago: as he had always been. He was just raising his head and sniffing a little suspiciously at the air.

'There is . . . something . . . Something here . . . eh?' He just said it, pronouncing the consonants sharply, and just thickening the vowels a bit, as they tend to do in Hanover. It had been exactly like that in the war, when we had wandered down the banks of the Danube, and thought there must be something there . . . But there never was.

I trotted along beside the other two, who were deep in animated conversation about Sweden and the countryside, about flying and Stockholm.

We had the Princess between us; sometimes we spoke over her head. I wallowed in their friendship.

To have someone to trust! To be with someone for a change who doesn't eye you suspiciously when you use a phrase that might perhaps offend his vanity, someone who isn't prepared at any moment to lower his visor and do battle with you to the death. Oh, people don't even argue like that – they squabble over one Mark fifty . . . over an old hat . . . over a bit of gossip . . . I know only two people in the whole world who would help me if I knocked on their doors at night and said: Gentlemen, this is my problem . . . I have to go to America – what shall I do? Two – Karlchen was one of them. Friendship is like one's homeland. We never talked about it, and whenever there was any slight surge of emotion unless it happened in a serious late-night talk – it would be quenched in a bucketful of colourful abuse. It was marvellous.

We had put him up at the hotel, because there were no rooms left where we were. He looked at his room, alleged that it stank like the bedroom of Louis the Smelly, and that it all seemed 'a bit thin' . . . but he said that about everything, and I had already picked up the habit from him; he washed, and then we sat and drank coffee under the trees.

'Well, Fritzchen . . .?' he said to me. No one will ever discover why he called me Fritzchen. 'Can you swim here? How's the lake?'

'It's generally about sixteen degrees Celsius or twenty Remius,' I said, 'depending on the currency fluctuations.'

He understood. 'And what are we doing tonight?'

'Well . . .' said the Princess, 'we're planning to have a very quiet evening . . .'

'Can you get red wine here?'

I reported on the depressing situation regarding red wine, and how at the *Sprit-Zentrale* a young man had looked for chablis among the red wines. Karlchen closed his eyes in sorrow. 'But you can get the wine, Karlchen – as the so-called down-payment for foreigners.' Unfortunately he didn't hear that. A girl went by – not even a particularly pretty one.

'Er . . .?' said Karlchen. 'Sorry, what . . .?' He carried on as if nothing had happened, and nothing *had* happened. But he had to say it – otherwise he might have burst. Gradually we began to behave like sensible people.

We had known each other a long time, and talked in a kind of abbreviated telegraphese. The Princess got the hang of it surprisingly quickly – but there was nothing secret about it, it was just our complete agreement on the basic issues of life. Both of us knew that 'things weren't that great' . . . and out of scepticism, understanding, inability and strength at the right time, we had produced an attitude that meant we kept quiet, where others set up a wild hubbub. Apart from his reliability, the man's great assets were negative: all the things he didn't say, didn't do, didn't start . . . We had none of those cultured, post-prandial conversations, in which men pay ghastly tribute to 'the spirit of the times', without actually changing their lives one iota. There was no dispensing of literary culture, and no Viennese aphorisms about

Death, Love, Life and Music, as you get from Austrian journalists and that ilk . . . it's terrifying listening, and the first time you hear it, you actually believe that printable twaddle, though there's not a word of truth in it. But Karlchen was a quiet sort. He blew smoke at the world, nothing surprised him, he was a steady worker at the Lord's filing-cabinet, and he brought up two children at home, while still remaining his own man. Now and again he would fall in love and sin, and when you asked him what he had done this time, he would bare his teeth in that typical grimace and say, 'She led me back over the threshold of youth!' and then everything would be all right again for a while.

Now he was sitting here, smoking and reflecting.

'We should write to Jakopp,' he said. Jakopp was the other one – there were three of us. Four, with the Princess.

'What shall we write?' I asked. 'Did you see him? You passed through Hamburg, didn't you?' Yes, Karlchen had passed through Hamburg and had seen him. Jakopp was the most crotchety of us. An employee of the Hamburg water-works, he was an orderly type with a passion for dahlias – 'the dahlia, an orderly flower', he would say – a playful and eccentric man, who had four hundred and forty-four *idées fixes* in his head. We were a good team.

'Where has the Princess got to?' asked Karlchen. The Princess had gone into town, 'buying buttons', in other words, shopping. We never went shopping together because whenever we did, we would squabble. She was gone, anyway. There was silence for a moment.

'Well, Karlchen, and apart from that?'

'Apart from that, Jakopp bought himself some pastilles because he smokes so much, and when he smokes, he coughs. You know how it is – a pretty disgusting sight. Now he's got something to stop him smoking: Fumasolan, the things are called.'

'Well? Are they any good?'

'Of course not. But he says that since he's started taking them, there's been a remarkable increase in his sexual powers. He resents it rather. Wonder if they gave him the wrong pastilles?'

Jakopp's life was always like that, and he gave us a lot of amusement.

'Give me a postcard. What shall we . . .?' At last I had the answer. We should send him a telegram-card, because a proper telegram was too expensive, although it would have had him delightfully confused and irritated. So from then on we cabled appallingly urgent messages on postcards – starting with the one today:

FLOWN OVER KARLCHEN ALMOST COMPLETELY ARRIVED WIRE IMMEDIATELY TO CONFIRM WILL WIRE STOP GRANNY SADLY FALLEN FROM SWING

GRANDAD

We finished the great work . . . and we were resting quietly from our labours, when the Princess arrived.

She had bought buttons of many kinds; it's quite bewildering what a multiplicity of wares a woman will find in even the smallest places. She had no money left either, so with a furrowed brow I pulled out my wallet and made rather a performance of it. Then we went and lay in the grass.

'Do you find it hard to relax, too?' asked Karlchen, who already felt completely at home. 'A holiday's hard work, I reckon. Even doing nothing is a big effort, and you only realise later quite how . . .?'

'Hm' we went; we were too lazy to answer. There was a rustle.

'Put that newspaper away!' I said.

'Did you read about . . .?' he said. And that did it: time had returned.

We had thought we could escape time. But you can't, it follows you. I looked at the Princess and pointed at the newspaper, and she nodded. We had talked about it the night before; about newspapers, about time in general, and about this time. One often thinks love is stronger than time; but time is always stronger than love.

'Reading . . . reading . . .' I said. 'Karlchen, what newspaper are you reading anyway?'

He told me the name.

'You shouldn't read just one,' I remarked sagaciously. 'That's no good. You have to read at least four newspapers, and one of the big French or English ones as well; things look very different seen from the outside.'

'I'm always amazed,' said the Princess, 'what people like us are offered – there aren't actually any newspapers for us. Those we do have, pretend we have God-knows how much money – no – they behave as if money didn't exist . . . but they know perfectly well we don't have much – they just pretend. The things they tell us . . . and the illustrations!'

'Just a jumble of fantasies. Go to sleep, go to sleep, go to sleep, dear child!'

'No, I don't mean that,' said the Princess. 'I mean they're always so terribly chic. Even when they write about being broke, they tell a stylish version of it. They seem to have both feet off the ground. Will a newspaper ever talk about what it's really like: how you start scrimping on the twentieth of each month, how things get miserable and petty sometimes, how you can rarely afford to take a taxi, not to mention buying a car. Instead, they feed us their ridiculous cult of fasionable living . . . do any of us live in proper flats?'

'Those people gobble you up,' I said. 'And the worst of it is that they set the questions. They mark out the course and build the fences – and you have to answer, and follow and jump . . . you can't choose for yourself. We're not on this planet to choose, but to make do – I know that. But you're just given a whole lot of crossword puzzles to solve: one from Rome, one from Russia, one from America; fashion and society and literature. It's a bit much for one man, I think.'

'If you think about it,' Karlchen said, 'we haven't really settled down since 1914. A bourgeois craving? I don't know. You achieve more when you have peace. An atmosphere lingers – effects go on being felt. Do you remember the insanity in people's eyes when our money melted away, and you could have bought the whole of Germany for a thousand dollars? We all wanted to be cowboys then. What a time!'

'My dear chap, it's our misfortune not to believe in so-called '"problems" – only fools console themselves with those. It's a parlour game.'

'Work,' said the Princess. 'Work helps.'

'Dear Princess,' said Karlchen, 'you women take what you do seriously – that's your undeniable advantage over the rest of us. But if you can't do that . . . and such a good-looking young woman too . . .'

'You'll be thrown out for that sort of talk,' said the Princess. 'Do you understand Platt German?'

Karlchen beamed: he spoke Platt like a Hanoverian farmer, and the two chattered away for a while in their foreign tongues.

What was that she said? I sat up. 'But you never told me that?'

'No? Didn't I?' The Princess was all innocence. Usually she was a good liar, but now she was terrible.

'Well?'

The Generalkonsul had been after her. When? Two months ago.

'Tell.'

'He was after me. Well, you all are. Sorry, Karlchen, all except you. One evening he . . . Well, it was like this. One evening he asked me if I could work late, he had a long "exposé" he wanted to dictate. That happens sometimes – I thought nothing of it; of course I stayed.'

'Of course . . .' I said. 'Otherwise you might even have an eight-hour day.'

'Leave it out, Poppa, of course we don't have it, I don't have it. In my position it's just . . .'

'We'll never agree on that, old girl. You don't have an eight-hour day, because you haven't fought for it. And you don't fight for it – oh, what the hell, I'm on holiday.'

'Are you agitators allowed holidays too?' asked Karlchen.

'Anyway,' the Princess continued, 'exposé. When it's done, he stops in the middle of the room – you know, Karlchen, my boss is terribly fat – stops in the middle of the room, looks at me with this strange expression and asks, Have you got a boyfriend? Yes, I say. Oh, he says, well there you are – and I thought you didn't have one. Why not? I say. You don't look as though, well, I mean . . . And gradually he comes out with it. He's so alone, I can see . . . at that moment he has no one at all, and he's had this girlfriend for years, but she's gone off with someone else.'

Karlchen shook his head unhappily, was such a thing possible.

'Well, and what did you say?'

'You great twit – I said no.'

'Oh?'

'Oh! Should I have said yes?'

'Well, who's to say! A good job . . . Oh by the way, I saw a film . . .'

'That's where he gets all his culture from, Karlchen. Now would you get into an affair with your boss?'

Karlchen said he would never get into an affair with his boss.

'It's no good,' the Princess said. 'Men never understand. What would be the point? I'd have to share his worries like a wife, work like his secretary, and then, when he feels he's safe, he'll stop in the middle of somebody else's room and ask her if she's got a boyfriend . . . No thanks!'

'And didn't you think of me at all?' I asked.

'No,' said the Princess, 'I only start thinking of you if the man's a possibility.' We got up and walked down to the lake.

The castle slept, quiet and satisfied. Everywhere, there was a smell of water and of wood that had been lying too long in the sun, and of fish and ducks. We walked along the shore of the lake.

I enjoyed the other two; one was a friend. No, they were both friends – and I didn't betray the woman for the man, as I had almost always done in the past; for when a man appeared, someone to talk to, then I dumped the woman, as though I hadn't just slept with her; I gave her up, didn't bother about her, and shamefully betrayed her to the first man who came along. Then she dropped me, and I wondered why.

The two of them were talking in their dialects about their respective regions. Where you had to pronounce the r and where not; they supplemented their stock of expletives; they both understood what lower German was about. Unfortunately, the German language hasn't taken up its style: how much more expressive it is, more colourful, simpler and clearer – the best love-poetry in German has been written in it. And the people . . .

the houses they had in old Lower Germany, particularly on the Baltic coast, were a dream-world of eccentricity, kindness and music, inhabited by an assortment of people like rare beetles, each one of them unique. A lot of its evocation has now fallen into the hands of stupid vernacular poets, may the devil take them, seemingly good-natured citizens with smoke-filled beards, brooding over steaming tankards, who have travestied the virility of their old language, and turned it into a deadly porridge of Gemütlichkeit: they are like head-foresters left in charge of the sea. Some have shaved off their beards and imagine they look like old woodcuts – but that doesn't help; they can't hear the woods or the sea, only their own beards rustling. Their good nature disappears the moment they turn confusedly to the present, and come up against political opposition; then the petit-bourgeois in them crawls out of the woodwork. Under their string vests, their hearts beat to the rhythm of a military parade.

That's not our Platt German, not that.

But Lower Germany will never die – it lives and will go on living, as long as Germany exists. There has only ever been one comparable culture outside Germany, and that existed on the backs of an ill-treated, oppressed people: in Courland. The Lower German is a different animal. He chooses his words carefully and well. This was what the two of them were talking about. I knew that all the best things about the Princess came from that soil. In her I loved a part of this country which is usually so hard to love, and whose bewildered spirits think it a distinction to be hated. And there was Time again. No, I suppose there are no holidays for us.

The two of them chattered away non-stop. Each of them claimed their own version of Platt German as the only true and fair one, the other's was entirely false. Now they had got around to telling stories.

The Princess told the one about the cobbler Hagen, to whom the administrator had called out his New Year's greeting: 'I wish you great happiness for the New Year, Master!' Whereupon the other had yelled respectfully back across the market-square, 'On the contrary, on the contrary, Herr Administrator!' And the one about Mayor Hacher who had brought his ox along to the show, and said, 'I'm not doing it for the money. I'm doing it for the disgrace!'

And then it was Karlchen's turn again. He told how Dörte, Mathilde and Zophie, the nosiest girls in the whole town of Celle, had asked him who the young man was, who was to be found wandering about the streets every morning. And how he'd then woken them up at night, which was easy enough, as they lived on the ground floor, and when all three of them came to the window, considerably alarmed, he said: 'I just wanted to tell you ladies that the morning visitor was a seller of holy books!'

And then they took it in turn to sing songs. The Princess sang:

'Old Mother Pietsche sits on Mount Sinai,
and when she's out of food, then she . . .

Karlchen, what about a little lullaby this afternoon?' she asked suddenly. Karlchen was just singing:

'She wore a brightly patterned dress,
and I'm still sore about the money I spent –

No,' he said. 'We'll have a nice walk in the afternoon. It'll do fatty here some good, and we'll all sleep better at night.'

Fatty was me. He gazed at me benevolently. 'Young people like you . . . you look so healthy and relaxed!'

That was how we felt too. I waddled along in silence beside them, because young love should be left to blossom.

Did he fancy her?

Of course he fancied her. But that was our unwritten law, our totem and taboo . . . We didn't know what star we had been born under; but it must have been the same one. Each other's women: never. We rationalised it like this: 'Your taste in women – no thanks all the same!' And again, for the hundredth time in as many years, I felt all the unspoken things in our friendship, the foundation on which it was built. I knew what made him tick. I knew it because I had seen all that the man had gone through ('I've had my share of storms,' he would say). I saw his unwavering self-control: when things went wrong he would keep a stiff upper lip. Often, when I was at a loss, I would ask myself what Karlchen would do. Then I'd be all right again for a time. A real male friendship . . . it's like an iceberg: only the last quarter of it is visible above the surface. The rest is submerged and invisible. Fun – but fun is only good when there's something serious behind it.

'Preaching in Platt German,' I heard Karlchen saying, 'no-no.'

'But that doesn't make sense, Herr Karlchen,' said the Princess. 'Why not? The peasants understand it much better. Not *your* Platt, of course . . . but ours . . .!'

'My beautiful young woman,' Karlchen said, 'that's not the point. The peasants would understand it, and for that reason they wouldn't like it. They don't want to hear their everyday language in church; they have no respect for it – where's the mystery in what they speak to their cows? They want the opposite, the formal, the unaccustomed. Otherwise they'll be disappointed and won't take the pastor seriously. There! And now we're going to the Café Chantant – remember that, Fritzchen?'

How could I forget! That was Herr Petkov from Rumania, from the time we had both played in the Rumanian theatre of war. Herr Petkov used to tell stories that were distinguished by their singular pointlessness, but they always wound up in a brothel. 'So he says to me: Petkov, you old bastard, let's go to the Chantant!' And what happened there, the Princess wanted to know.

Karlchen explained: 'Petkov used to slap his thighs and say: here a girl and there a girl . . .'

'Karlchen,' said the Princess, 'you're making me blush!'

'Petkov had a girlfriend too. She must have had a dozen lovers before him.'

'A dozen lovers,' said the Princess appraisingly, 'and how many loose men?'

We walked along. The Princess stopped to powder her nose.

'I can't understand how you can powder your face in God's own Nature,' I said. 'The fresh air . . . and your complexion is . . .'

'Go and win the Nobel Prize and shut up!' she said.

'But listen, I'm serious . . .'

'Poppa, it's something men will never understand, and yet the two of us get along very well. Each to his own, cheri. You don't use make-up, and I'm partial to a little powder. That's how it is!'

We sat down on a bench.

I growled, 'They're all the same . . .' a sentence of Byron's that made up half my entire stock of English.

'Be nice to her for a change,' said Karlchen. The Princess was delighted and gave him a friendly nod.

'That's right!'

'Treat your bride as a woman, and your woman as a bride!' said Karlchen.

'Now give each other a kiss!' I said.

They did.

'Be nice to her!' Karlchen said again. He was only passing through. Men in that position can always be clever and gentle, they have kind and wise words for every situation, and then they move on. But we who have to stay . . . But then that little cloud blew over. Because Karlchen quoted a good proverb to us:

'At home they always say: It takes more than four bare legs in bed to make a marriage.'

'Karlchen,' I said abruptly, 'what will become of us? I mean later . . . when we're old . . .?'

He didn't answer immediately. Instead it was the Princess who spoke: 'Poppa, you remember what it said on the old clock we saw together in Lübeck, and which we couldn't afford to buy just then?'

'Yes,' I said. 'It said, Let the years speak for themselves.'

When we got home, we found a large bouquet for the Princess, of carrots, parsley and celery. It was from Karlchen, because that was how he showed his love.

2

'Just wait till Frau Direktor sees that!' said the maid Emma. 'She's already in a right temper today!'

The laughter of the four girls died on their lips. One bent down timidly to pick up the books they had just been throwing at one

73

another. Hanne, fat Hanne from East Prussia, started to ask, 'What is it? Is Frau Direktor . . .?'

'Never mind!' said the maid, with a malicious laugh. 'You'll see!' And she hurried away. The four stood together a moment longer, then scattered hurriedly into the corridor. Hanne was last.

She had just opened the door of the dormitory where all the others were, collecting their bathing-things, when they heard Frau Adriani's shrill voice from downstairs – how loud it must be, to be heard so clearly! The girls stood rigid like wax dolls.

'Ha! So you didn't know? Our little Lieschen didn't know! Haven't I told you a thousand times not to leave cupboards open? What? Ha?' You could hear very soft, muffled crying. Upstairs the girls looked at each other and gasped; they thrilled with fear.

'You're a slut!' said the distant voice. 'A dirty slut! What? The cupboard opened by itself? Well I never . . . And what's this? Eh? Since when have you been keeping food with your clothes? Eh? You limb of Satan! I'll teach you . . .'

The crying grew louder; so loud, it could now be heard distinctly. They couldn't hear any blows – Frau Adriani didn't beat, she cuffed.

'There – and there – and now . . . I'll teach the pack of you . . .' Fortissimo: 'Everybody downstairs! Into the dining-hall!'

The wax dolls came to life; they threw their bathing-things onto their beds, their faces suddenly flushed, and one of them, pale Gertie, had tears in her eyes. Then there was another swift command, 'Get along with you! Quick!' and they went downstairs, almost at a run, in silence.

The girls poured out of every door; they wore frightened expressions, one quietly asked, 'What's the matter . . .' and was immediately silenced by the others; in a thunderstorm, it was best not to talk. Feet clattered down the stairs, doors banged . . . now the dining-hall was full. Last of all came Frau Adriani like a red cloud, with a crying Lisa Wedigen in tow.

The woman's face was bright red. Only when she was in such a state of excitement was she fully alive.

'Everybody present?' She surveyed the assembled girls with a look that seemed to single out each girl as its object. Then she said harshly, 'Lisa Wedigen has been stealing food!'

'I . . .' but the girl's sobs choked what she was trying to say.

'Lisa Wedigen is a thief. She has stolen our food,' Frau Adriani said emphatically. 'Stolen it, and then hidden it away in her cupboard. Of course the cupboard was in a disgraceful state, as always happens with thieves; her clothes were soiled with food, and the cupboard door was left open. So, as you clearly haven't bothered to listen, I'll have to make you understand. You remember what I told you at the beginning: if any of you mis-behaves, you will all be punished for it. I'll show you . . .! Right: Lisa will get no supper. For the next week she won't be allowed to go on walks with the rest of us, she will have to stay in her room. Tomorrow she will get only half-helpings. Bathing has been cancelled today. You will all have writing-practice instead. And Lisa will copy out four chapters from the Bible. You're an evil lot! Right, march – up to your rooms!'

In silence and with heavy hearts, the children trickled out through the two doors, some exchanged significant looks, the tougher ones swung their arms and acted defiant and uncon-cerned; two were crying. Lisa Wedigen was sobbing, she looked at no one and no one looked at her. The child looked up.

The big calendar-pad on the wall showed a 27, a black 27. As the child pushed through the doorway with the others, a draught leafed through the calendar . . . so many leaves, so many days. And when this calendar was used up, Frau Adriani would hang up another one. The child's eye fell on the painting of Gustavus Adolphus in the corridor. He was all right. He was here and yet he wasn't here. No one did anything to him. Strange, how people don't hurt things. Another day like this, thought the child, and I'll run away, away from this house . . .

There was quiet activity in the rooms. Bathing-costumes and towels were put away, trembling hands opened drawers and hastily rummaged about in them, the odd whisper was heard.

Down in the dining-hall, Frau Adriani stood alone.

She was breathing rapidly. To begin with she had coldly worked herself into a rage – for a pedagogical purpose, so she thought – and now she was purely and simply raging. Her fury only abated when she recalled her recent performance. She'd had such an attentive audience . . . everything depended on having an audience. She looked about herself. Everything here, down to the plaster on the walls, the putty in the window-frames, the lino floor and the door-hinges – everything was counted, checked, listed and supervised. There was nothing here that was not subject to her rule. She felt that if she glared at the fireplace, the fire would burn more quietly. This was her empire. It was for this reason that Frau Adriani didn't like going out with the children; she spoiled their walks in any way she could, because nature wouldn't stand to attention for her. Her will rampaged through the spacious villa, which had long ceased to be an ordinary house as far as she was concerned – it was her absolute domain, a world apart. Her world. She kneaded the children. Every day, she moulded her forty children, her servants, her nieces – her husband didn't count. She played excruciatingly pleasurable games with these live figures, and continually checkmated them. Her will always prevailed. There was no secret behind her success: she believed in her victory, she could work like a carthorse, and she didn't waste her emotions on others.

She thought she was unique, Frau Adriani. But she had brothers and sisters all over the world.

3

It was a bright summer's day – and we were very glad. In the morning the clouds had dispersed quickly; now the wind dropped, and large white tufts of cotton wool gleamed high up in the blue sky, leaving at least half of it uncovered and dark-blue – and there was the sun, rejoicing.

'We're not having a nap today either,' said Karlchen, who remarkably didn't want to sleep after lunch. 'Instead we'll go for a walk in the fields. Right!'

Away we went. Peasants passed us, we greeted them, and they answered something we didn't understand.

'Don't learn the Swedish for everything!' said the Princess. 'If you speak a foreign language perfectly, then it stops being so much fun. The Tree of Knowledge isn't always the Tree of Life.'

'Lydia,' I said, 'let's go past the children's home this time!'
We did.

Down the avenue and round the lake. Once a car came reeling towards us, there was no other way of putting it, it was moving in a zig-zag.

A young man was at the wheel, with that silly, strained expression of learner-driver. His teacher sat next to him. We leapt out of the way, because the young man would have run over the three of us as easily as running over an ant . . . We left the avenue and turned into the wood.

In Sweden, paths sometimes take you directly through small properties, a gate is left open, and you pass through the yard. There were little cottages, quiet and clean . . .

'Look – that'll be the children's home over there!' said Karlchen.

On a little hill was a long house-front; that was it. Slowly we approached it. Everything was very peaceful. We stopped.

'Tired?' We lay down on the moss and rested. A long, long time.

Suddenly a door slammed in the house – it was like a pistol shot. Quiet. The Princess raised her head.

'I wonder if we'll get to see their strict teacher . . .' I didn't finish my sentence. A small door had opened at the side of the house, and a little girl flew out. She was running blind. No, like an animal; she didn't need to look where she was going – she was driven by instinct. First of all, she ran straight ahead, then she looked up, and with a lightning movement, she swerved and ran straight into our arms.

'There . . . there,' I went.

The child looked up: as if waking from a long sleep. Her mouth opened and closed again, her lips trembled, she didn't speak. Now I recognised her: we had met her with the others on our walk.

'Well . . .?' said the Princess. 'You are in a hurry . . . where are you off to. Playing?'

At that, the little girl's head dropped, and she began to cry . . . I had never heard anything like it. Women are less lyrical than we men are, when confronted with pain, so they are more helpful.

The Princess bent over her. 'What is it ... what's the matter?' and wiped her tears away. 'What is it? Who's hurt you?'

The child sobbed. 'I ... she ... I've already run away once today ... Frau Direktor ... Lisa Wedigen stole something, she wants to beat me, she wants to beat us all, I won't get any supper – I want my Mummy! I want my Mummy!'

'Where is your Mummy?' asked the Princess.

The little girl didn't answer; she looked anxiously over at the house and made as if to run away.

'Now just you stay here with us – what's your name?'

'Ada,' said the little girl.

'And what else?'

'Ada Collin.'

'And where is your Mummy?'

'Mummy ...' said the child, and then something we couldn't make out.

'Does your Mummy live here usually?'

The child shook her head.

'Where then?'

'In Switzerland. In Zurich ...'

'Well?' I asked. Only a man could have asked such a stupid question. The child didn't even look up; she hadn't understood there was a question. We stood around, rather at a loss.

'Why did you run away – now tell me the whole story properly. All of it ...' the Princess began again.

'Frau Adriani hits us ... she gave us no food today ... I want to go to Mummy ... I want to go to Mummy ...!'

Karlchen, as ever, thought quickly and clearly. 'Let's take down where her mother lives,' he said.

'Tell me,' asked the Princess, 'where does your mother live?'

The child gulped. 'In Zurich!'

'Yes, I know, but where in Zurich? ...'

'In Hott ... Hott ... she's coming ... she's coming!' screamed the child, and tore herself away. We held her back and looked up.

The front door of the house had opened, and a red-haired

woman strode up to us. 'What are you doing with that child?' she asked, without any preliminaries.

I took my hat off. 'Good afternoon!' I said politely.

The woman didn't even look at me. 'What are you up to with that child? What is the child doing here?'

'She ran out of the house, and came here crying,' said Karlchen.

'The child is good for nothing. She's run away once already today. Give her to me and don't concern yourself with things that are none of your business!'

'Now just a minute,' I said. 'The child came here crying; she says you hit her.'

The woman looked at me aggressively. 'Me? I didn't beat her. No children are beaten here. I have parental authority over the children, and I have it in writing. How dare you? I keep a disciplined and orderly establishment . . . I don't want you inciting the children against me! That's *my* house!' she suddenly screamed and pointed at the building.

'That may be so,' I said, 'but there's something wrong here – the girl comes running up to us scared to death . . .'

The woman made a grab for the child, tiny points of flame blazing in her green eyes.

'You're coming with me now,' she said to the child. 'Straight away! And you're clearing off! Now!'

'It would be nice if you would speak a little more civilly,' said Karlchen.

'I'm not talking to you anyway,' said the woman.

The Princess had bent down again, and was wiping the tears off the child's pale, drained face.

'What are you whispering to the child?' screamed the woman. 'You're not to whisper. You aren't responsible for her, I am. I am the headmistress here – I am! I!' Those blazing eyes . . . She radiated heat.

'I think we'll let the lady – ' said Karlchen. The woman grabbed at the child again, she tore at her as if she were a thing; I sensed it wasn't the girl who was at stake, so much as her power over the girl. The child was green with fear, she was being pulled along behind her; no one said anything. They had reached the house. I gestured feebly, as if to stop them . . . the two disappeared through the big door, the door closed, a key grated in the lock. It was all over.

There we stood.

'How about that . . .' said Karlchen. The Princess put away her handkerchief.

'You're a pair of prize idiots!' she said forcefully.

'All right,' I said, 'but why?'

'Come with me.'

We went a little way into the wood.

'You . . .' said the Princess. 'We can't just fight it out, I do see that. But we want to help the child, don't we? Well, and so what's the mother's name?'

'Collin. Frau Collin.' I said very proudly.

'Right – and how do you want to help?' She was right. We didn't have the address. Zurich . . . Zurich . . . what else had the child said?

The Princess continued, 'I whispered to her that we would pass the house in half an hour, and she was to try to get the address to us on a bit of paper. I'm sure it won't work – the poor child is so petrified as it is. But we'll see . . . What an old dragon, though! She really does spit fire!'

'Magnificent woman,' said Karlchen. 'There's someone I'd like to marry! I mean . . . what I mean is . . .'

'Let's go and lie down in the meadow for a while,' said the Princess.

'Did you see that, Karlchen,' I said, 'the woman's hair was standing on end! I've never seen anything like it . . .'

'You can put as much make-up as you like on your bum, but you can't turn it into a face. That woman . . .'

'Quiet!' said the Princess. We listened. From the house, some distance away now, came the sound of a high scolding voice. We couldn't hear what was being said, we could only hear someone shouting angrily. My blood rose. Perhaps she was beating the child.

'Pah!' muttered Karlchen. The meadow disappeared and the Princess' deep alto reached me as through a haze.

'We'll go straight to the house afterwards . . . we have to . . .'

An enormous oval ring, under a stone vaulting, taut red cloths; at the bottom, the arena, then a high stone wall, and over that the first rows of spectators, tier upon tier of them, thousands of heads until they blurred into the brown light at the back. Down in the middle was a man on a cross; a panther was leaping up at him, and tearing away one piece of flesh after another ... The man didn't scream, his head had lolled onto his left shoulder, he was probably already unconscious. Dust and the roar of the crowd ... A small lattice door opened: a couple of men in leather aprons pushed some trembling figures, four men and a woman, ahead of them into the ring. Three of the men were in rags; the woman was half-naked, and the last man wore make-up and – a hideous mask and tinsel crown: an actor in his own death scene. The little lattice door was closed from inside. The men stayed behind it, professional spectators. A few animals had been lying in the sand off to one side, a tiger, a lion. When they saw the people being driven into the arena, they got up, lazy and evil. One of the four had a weapon – a curved sword. The panther had abandoned the man on the cross; he now lay, chewing a torn-off arm. The blood dripped.

Suddenly the lion tensed to leap; he was enraged, because somebody from a safe place above him had dropped a burning ember on his head. The lion roared. The gladiator approached.

His movement, intended to be heroic, merely looked pathetic. A tuba shrilled with a red sound. The lion leapt. He leapt right over the gladiator, onto the man in make-up. He seized him – the mask's foolish expression never changing – and dragged him screaming across the sand. A couple of tigers had attacked the gladiator. He resisted strongly, with the courage of desperation; laying about himself, first according to some plan he had, and then wildly. One of the animals moved to outflank him, it stepped back on noiseless paws, and then they were both on him. The shock went through the entire circus. 'Rragh,' went the crowd, groaning as one. The spectators had jumped out of their seats. They gazed enraptured, their eyes darting everywhere so as not to miss a single detail, and wherever they looked there was blood, desperation, groaning and roaring – people suffering, living flesh convulsed and writhing to death in the sand – while they were high up, in safety. It was marvellous! The whole circus was awash with cruelty and delirium. Only the lowest rows sat quietly and a little haughtily, apparently unmoved. They were the senators and their wives, vestal virgins, the court, high-ranking officers and rich patricians . . . sedately they offered one another sweetmeats in little pots, one of them straightened his toga. Shouts incited the animals, and whipped them up to still greater rage; shouts rained down on the cowardly fighter who had been incapable of defending himself . . . Shouting and sweating, the crowd was an animal rolling in an orgasm of pleasure. It gave birth to cruelty. What was happening here was one gigantic and shameless procreative act of destruction. It was a lust for negation – the sweet slide into death, for the contestants. And it was for this that they spent day after day weaving sandals, inscribing parchment, fetching mortar, paying calls on the nobility and waiting out long mornings in the atrium; weaving cloth and washing linen, painting terracotta and selling stinking fish . . . in order at last, at long last, to enjoy this great public holiday in the amphitheatre. Everything, absolutely everything that their daily routine had ground into these citizens and proles in the way of humiliation and oppression, of stifled fantasies and unsatisfied lusts, could spend itself here. It was like sexual gratification, only more violent, hotter and more explosive. The pleasure of four thousand people soared up like a dart of fire – they were one body, driving itself to exhaustion, they were both the predators and the humans being ripped apart down there. Atrocity opened their eyes – something for which every century has found a different name. They were panting, the wildest spurt was over, now what was left spilled out in noisy raucous conversation. They shouted and gestured over each other's heads, their thumbs-down, a thousand voices were heard, shouting and speaking, and only here and there the faint sound of a cry, a signal-whistle of pain. What flowed away here was the pent-up criminal longings of these people. They would commit fewer murders now; the animals had done it for them. Afterwards, they went into the temples to pray. No, to entreat. Below, the first guards went out onto the sand and set about the bodies with hot irons – were they properly dead? Had they not cheated the crowds of some tiny ounce of pain? In one corner someone was twitching away his final seconds of agony, while the animals, replete but still excited, disappeared through the small grille doors. The sand was swept, and above, in the gods, the last swell of delight at this suffering boiled away.

'What's the matter?' asked the Princess.

'Nothing,' I said.

'You think we should really go to the house again?' Karl asked doubtfully.

'Of course we should,' said the Princess. 'The child needs help. We have to help her.'

I felt a surge of emotion, such a dull fury that I had to get up and take a deep breath – the other two watched me in astonishment. Suddenly I felt the same pleasure in destruction, in the suffering of others; to make that woman suffer . . . Oh the joy of the righteous Crusade, purge of immorality! I quenched it with a jet of cold air as I breathed out. I understood all too well the workings of that pleasure: it was doubly dangerous, because it had an ethical basis; torture, for a worthwhile end . . . a widespread ideal.

'Shall we go?'

When we saw the house again, we fell silent as though in response to a command.

'One of us go left, another round the back,' said Karlchen.

'But someone has to stay with the Princess,' I said. 'That woman would be perfectly capable of hitting her.'

'Then you go that way,' he said. 'I'll try the left.' We crept nearer.

The house was quiet, very quiet. Was she watching us from a window? What if she had a dog? Whatever else, it was private property; we had no business here. The woman had the law on her side. What a Prussian way of thinking! A child was suffering. Go.

Everything was quiet. From here you could see a long way into the countryside beyond the house. There was Lake Maelar, there was Castle Gripsholm, red, with its thick domes, and the mixed wood of birch and fir.

'Pst!' hissed the Princess. Nothing. Karlchen was out of sight. I looked at her questioningly. We continued slowly, treading carefully as if on thin ice. Was that a face in a window – a circular window . . .? Wrong, it was a reflection. We passed very close to the house. The Princess looked all round her. Suddenly she moved forward. 'Quick!' she said. She ran up to a white patch in the grass not far from the house . . . it was a little piece of paper. At the back of the house, Karlchen was making his way slowly along the fence. The Princess bent down, looked at the paper, picked it up and walked on smartly.

We hurried to get out of danger.

'Well?' said Karlchen. The Princess stopped and read out from the paper, 'Collin Zurich Hottingerstrase 104'.

The back of a leaf from a calendar, in a scrawly child's hand. 'Strase' with a single 's'. 'That's that then!' said the Princess.

Karlchen whistled a march. We started back to Gripsholm.

4

We ran around in confusion like Red Indians on the warpath. All three of us spoke at once.

'Now slow down,' said clever Karlchen. 'A telegram . . . you must be mad. What we do now is write her a sensible letter. Saying . . .'

What happened then . . . I wouldn't like to have to go through that again. It was a battle. Not *one* letter was written – but fourteen, one after another, then three at a time, with the other two covering sheet after sheet of paper, while I bashed away on my typewriter till it glowed. It was like one of those old-fashioned parlour-games ('What does he do? What does she do? Where did they meet?'). Each of us wanted to read his own out first, and each thought his own composition by far the best and most suitable, and those of the others completely out of the question.

'Out of the question!' said the Princess.

'That's pure kids' stuff!' I wanted to reply.

'You're so clever,' she said, 'you're tying yourself in fancy knots! Now do me a favour . . .' and the whole thing began all over again.

In the end, there were three versions left in the running. Karlchen had written a lawyer's letter. I had written a subtle and refined one, and the Princess a clever one, so we chose hers.

Simply and clearly, it told what we had seen, and that we didn't mean to interfere in the Collin's family affairs and that she shouldn't write to Adriani herself, as this would only lead to more trouble. It told her that she wasn't to be alarmed, and in the meantime we would see what steps might be taken – but if she would permit us to telephone her once.

'There,' said the Princess and sealed the letter. 'That's that done. Now let's post it straight away!' It was a weight off all our minds when the letter landed in the letter-box.

'A girl like that . . .' I said. 'Poor little thing!' And they both laughed at me.

'Give us a cigarette!' said Karlchen, who liked smoking other people's and using their toothpaste. ('Friendship should be put to use,' he would say.) 'You remember, don't you,' he said into the evening silence as we strolled through the streets of Mariefred, looking at the shop-windows, 'that I'm leaving tomorrow night?' Bang! We'd forgotten. Yes – the week was up.

'Won't you stay with us a little longer, Karling?' asked the Princess.

'Madam,' replied the lanky layabout and stretching out an arm, 'unfortunately my holiday is coming to an end – I must. Ladies and gentlemen, that was a most exhausting conference!' He stopped. 'Well, you're the expert on conferences . . . you civil servant.'

'I don't call you a writer either, chum. Old Eugen Ernst always used to say, whenever someone's got nothing to do, he gets hold of some other people and they hold a conference. And at the end, when they've all spoken, there is a statement. Then it's finished. Now, back to the typing grindstone and let's have another telegram-postcard for Jakopp!' I obeyed.

'I think,' I said to Karlchen, 'it had better be a one-word telegram. It'll be too expensive otherwise. There:

WIREIMMEDIATELYIFINTENDPURCHASINGLOCALLAKEMAELAR-
FORWATERINGWATERGUARANTEEDGENUINETHOUGHFOR-

SWIMMINGPURPOSESONLYALMOSTRESPECTFULLY-
FRITZCHENANDKARLCHENHEADWATERCOMMISSIONERS.'

'Well, and now shall we concoct a farewell drink?' asked
Lydia. We ran around and pestered the good lady of the castle
for something to drink; we went shopping, but none of it seemed
quite good enough; we unwrapped what we'd got and laid it out.
'What is there to eat?' enquired Karlchen.
'What would you like?' asked the Princess.
'What I really feel like is some marmot's tail soup.'
'Some what?'
'Don't you know it? Young folks nowadays! In my day . . .
Well, marmot's tail soup is procured in the Far North by
Eskimos. They pursue the marmot until it drops its tail in fright,
and in this way . . .'
We flung a couple of cushions at him, and went downstairs to
eat.
'I'd really like to travel via Ulm,' said Karlchen. 'There is a
young lady I have to see – I'd like to check up on her.'
'You should be ashamed of yourself!' said the Princess.
'Is she good-looking?' I asked. 'Well, hardly, I suppose . . .
your women . . .'
He grinned – and in the circumstances, was unable to say:
What about yours . . .
'How do you plan to go via Ulm?' I asked. 'It's right out of
your way!'
'I'm not going there,' said Karlchen. 'I'd just like to . . .'
'A proper Casanova,' said the Princess. 'Careful, woman,' I
said, 'sometimes he suits the action to the words, and then things
get pretty lively.'
Karlchen smiled, as though it was some entirely unrelated
wild man who was being spoken of, and we uncorked a bottle of
whisky with an extremely audible 'Pop!', whereupon Karlchen
was nicknamed 'Herr Popper'. We sat and drank in great
moderation. We talked ourselves drunk. Our four candles flick-
ered in the breeze.
'Smoke your pipe!' said Karlchen. 'Go on, smoke it! He can't
take nicotine, Princess! Is it a new pipe?'

'That's the trouble,' I said, 'I have to break it in . . .'

'Aren't there machines for that?' asked the Princess. 'I've heard of something like that.'

'Yes, there are,' said Karlchen. 'I had a friend at school who discovered a way of using an air-pump to break in a pipe. I can't remember how he did it – but he did. I gave him my new pipe, a wonderful new pipe. And he must have pumped at it a bit too strongly . . . and the pipe smoked itself, and there was nothing left of it but a little pile of ashes. He had to buy me a new one. That story always seemed very symbolic to me . . . Yes, but I forget what it symbolised.' We remained silent, lost in thought.

'An ass!' said the Princess. We wanted to protest, but she was referring to a real one, which had just appeared from behind some trees. He was probably after some whisky too. We got up at once and stroked him, but asses don't like being stroked; a wise man discovered that it was their misfortune to be called asses, and that was the only reason why they were so badly treated. We treated this one well and called him Joachim. We played the gramophone for him . . .

'Play a bit from *Carmen*,' said the Princess. 'No! Play the one with the little gnomes . . .!' That was a piece of music with a little skipping-marching rhythm, and the Princess insisted it was meant to go with a pantomime in which dwarves with little lanterns scampered across the stage. I put on the record with the gnomes, the machine did its stuff, the ass ate grass and we drank whisky.

'Another finger for me please!' said Karlchen.

For dessert the Princess was eating celery and cheese, as a great gourmet had recommended.

'What's it like?' asked Karlchen.

'It tastes,' the Princess chewed slowly and thoughtfully – 'it tastes like dirty laundry.' Even Joachim swished his tail about in disapproval.

Then we sang him all the songs we knew, and there were a considerable number of them.

'King Solomon has three hundred wives
and that's the reason why
he always missed his morning train
kissing them all good-bye!'

'Mooh!' went the ass, and was given a talking to – after all, he wasn't a cow. Karlchen blew some gentle melodies on a comb-and-tissue-paper, and boisterously expressed a desire to go to the Chantant . . . the Princess laughed a lot, and sometimes at an undignified volume, and, like both of the others, I was convinced I was the only one left sober in the midst of this hullaballoo.

Before we went to bed, I said, 'Lydia – he's not to write postcards this time! He keeps writing postcards!'

'What kind . . .?' she asked.

'When he leaves, the craziest postcards arrive the next day, he writes them on the train. It's his way of saying goodbye. He's not to; it worries me!'

'Herr Karlchen, will you swear not to write any postcards?'

He gave us his word of honour as a citizen of Giessen. We hit the sack.

The next evening we took him to the station, to the little puffing railway train, and the two of them gave each other a farewell kiss that seemed to me to take rather a long time. Then he had to get on, and we stood beside the little carriage, giving him good advice for the journey. He bared his teeth at us and when the train started to move, he said agreeably, 'Fritzchen, I've taken your toothpaste with me!' In my excitement I threw my hat after him, and it almost rolled under the wheels. He waved, and then the little train disappeared round the corner, and we couldn't see anything any more.

At noon the next day, four postcards arrived: one from each of the main stations on the way to Stockholm. On the last one he had written the following:

'Dear Toni!
On no account let the police take you in for questioning over the false entry at the hotel on the 15th! If need be, remain firm and insist you are my daughter!

Dear friend, before I left this evening, I looked at your profile once more and I must say I was seriously alarmed. I believe you're losing your hair. That's more than an indication – that's a symptom!

Don't search in vain for the second canary – I've taken it home for my dear little children. Where is the ass?

Dear Marie, please look at once for my signet-ring – it must be under your pillow. I know it for a fact.

Pity about my wasted holiday!

I am evermore
your dear
Karlchen.'

Chapter Four

So long as our pastor doesn't see me,
I'll take my chances with God, said the peasant –
and he made his hay on a Sunday.

I

'How did all that come about so suddenly?' asked the Princess, as I toppled out of my head-stand.

We were doing exercises, Lydia was, I was – and over there, Billie was rolling about under the trees. Billie wasn't a man, but a young woman by the name of Sibylle.

'Oh boy . . .' said the Princess and dropped onto the ground, gasping for breath. 'If that doesn't make us clever and beautiful . . .'

'And slim,' I said, and sat down next to her.

'How do you like her?' asked the Princess, with a nod over at the trees.

'I like her,' I said. 'She's a nice girl: fun, playful, serious when she wants to be. Such a sweetheart!'

'Who?'

'Her.'

'Talking of hearts, Poppa, she's just broken up with her boyfriend, but discreetly and amicably.'

'And who was he again?'

'The painter. A decent young man. It just didn't work any more. Don't ask her, she doesn't want to talk about it. It's the kind of thing you have to cope with on your own.'

'How long have you known each other?'

'Oh, ten years and more. Billie . . . she's like Karlchen to me, you know? I like her. And a man has never come between us. I just can't imagine that ever happening. Look at her, the way she runs! As if her pants are on fire!'

Sibylle came over.

I liked watching her run; she had long legs, a firm torso, and her dark-blue swimsuit glowed against the green of the grass.

'Well, you monkeys?' said Billie and sat down with us. 'How was it?'

'Profitable,' said the Princess. 'Fatty here did some exercises, his knees will be coming through the back of his neck any minute ... he's been very good. How long have you been skipping now?'

'Three minutes,' I said very proudly. 'How did you sleep, Miss Billie?'

'Quite well. At first, when the woman got the small room ready for us, I thought it might be too hot, with the sun shining in there all day, but it wasn't really that hot at all. So I slept quite well.'

We all looked attentively ahead, and swayed to and fro.

'It's great that you've come,' said the Princess, and tickled the back of Billie's neck very gently with a long blade of grass. 'We were going to live here like a couple of hermits – but then first his friend Karlchen arrived, and now you – but it's so quiet and peaceful ... no, honestly ...'

'How kind of you Ma'am,' said Billie and laughed.

I loved her laugh; sometimes it was silvery, but sometimes there was a dovelike quality about it – a cooing laugh.

'What a pretty ring, Billie,' I said.

'It's nothing ... a little everyday ring ...'

'Show me ... an opal? Opals ... you know ... opals are unlucky!'

'Not for me, Herr Peter, not for me. Should I wear a diamond instead?'

'Of course you should. And then you can use it to scratch your name in the mirror of your *chambre séparée*. That's what all great cocottes do.'

'Thanks. By the way, Walter said he'd been in a *cabinet particulier* in Paris too, and someone had scratched something on the mirror there. Guess what it said!'

'Well?'

'*Vive l'anarchie!* I thought that was great.' We were pleased.

'Shall we gymnase a bit more?' I asked.

'Not for me, thanks,' said the Princess and stretched. 'I've done my bit. Billie, your swimsuit's coming undone!' She buttoned it up for her.

Billie had a tan, either permanently, or from the sun by the seaside where she had been before. As well as her brown skin, she had fawn-coloured eyes and, amazingly, blonde hair, real blonde . . . it didn't seem to go with the rest of her. Billie's mother was a . . . a what? From Pernambuco. No, her mother was German, she had lived in Pernambuco a long time with her German husband, and there must have been something once upon a time . . . Billie was, at a cautious guess, a half-caste, or a half-half-caste, something like that. There was a foreign sweetness about her; when she sat like that, with her legs drawn up, her hands behind her knees, she was like a beautiful cat. You could watch her forever.

'What sort of schnaps was it we drank last night?' Billie asked slowly, without taking her eyes off what was happening at a distance accessible only to herself. The question was perfectly valid – but her expression was wrong for it, a quietly dreamy rigidity, and then out came that question about schnaps . . . We laughed. She awoke. 'Well . . .' she said.

'It was a Labommel schnaps,' I said perfectly seriously.

'No, really . . . what was it?'

'It was a Swedish corn brandy. If you only have a glass of it as we did, it's pleasant and refreshing.'

'Yes, very pleasant . . .' We were silent again, and enjoyed the sun. The wind breathed over us, fanning our skin and stroking our glowing pores. I was in a minority, but I didn't mind. The two were united – not against me, but to some extent excluding me. For all our affection, as I walked along beside them, I suddenly felt that ancient childish feeling little boys sometimes have, that women are strange, alien beings whom you will never understand. The way they are made, what they have under their skirts . . . just the way they are! My boyhood coincided with a time when women's rigging was something highly complicated – just think off all those hooks and buttons to be done up when they got dressed! Adultery must have been an intricate business then. Nowadays, men have more buttons than women, who, if they are clever, can open as simply as a zip-fastener. And sometimes, when I hear women talking together, I think each must know the secret of the other; they are subject to the same manipulations and fluctuations in their existence, they have children in the same way . . . People are always saying women hate each other. Perhaps it's because they know each other so well? They know too much about one another, right down to their essential being, which for many of them is the same thing. The rest of us probably have a harder time of it.

There they were, sitting in the sun, chatting, and I felt content. It was rather like a eunuch's contentment; if I'd been proud, I might have said a Pasha's – but it wasn't that at all. I felt so secure in their presence. Billie had been with us for four days, and in those four days we hadn't had a single wrong moment together . . . it was all lightness and happiness.

'What was he like?' I heard the Princess ask. 'The soles of his feet and the parting in his hair were a gentleman's,' said Sibylle, 'but in between . . .' I didn't know whom they were talking about – I had just picked up the tail end.

'Oh nonsense!' said the Princess. 'If a man is no good, you should leave him as fast as you can. As for that woman, she must be so stupid to stand for it. Oh well! Hey, look! Ssh! Sit quietly – then he'll come nearer . . . Look at the way his tail bobs about!' A little bird hopped up to us, inclined his head to one side, and then flew off, alarmed by something in his brain – we hadn't moved.

'What kind of bird was that?' Billie asked.

'That was a bulbulfinch,' said the Princess.

'Come on, silly – that wasn't a bullfinch . . .' said Billie.

'I'll tell you something,' I lectured. 'With those sort of answers it doesn't matter if they're right or not. They just have to be prompt! Jakopp told me once, how when their group went on an excursion, there was always one who was the information-wallah. He had to know everything. And when he was asked, What's that building? He had to say, and quick, that's the District Savings Bank of Lower Saxony! He didn't have the faintest, but everyone was satisfied: the gap had been filled. That's how it is.'

The girls smiled politely, and suddenly I was alone with my joke. Just a split second, then it was over. They got up.

'Let's have a race!' said Billie. 'Once round the meadow! Ready, steady – go!'

We ran. Billie led; she ran evenly, her well-trained body worked like a precise little machine . . . it was a joy to run with her. Behind me the Princess gasped occasionally. 'Keep calm!' I said to myself. 'Breathe through your nose – use the whole of your foot – not too much spring!' We ran on. Billie let out a long breath and stopped; we had gone almost once round the big meadow.

'Whew!' We were very hot. 'The castle, and a shower!' We took our bathing wraps and walked slowly over the meadow. I carried my gym shoes in my hand, and the grass tickled my feet. It's good being with the girls, without any tension. Without tension?

2

'What shall we take the child as a present?'

'Sweets,' suggested Billie.

'No,' I said, 'the old woman won't allow it – or she'll have to share them out among the whole house.'

'We'll go and buy some buttons,' said the Princess. 'I'm sure I'll find something. Come on, Billie! Forget about my hat!' We went.

Frau Collin had written. She was very grateful to us, and we should go to Frau Adriani and talk with her, and then report back on the telephone. The expenses . . .

'Not *huddan*! *Ladi*!' shouted the Princess. Billie looked flummoxed, and I had to explain to her that that meant 'left' and 'right' – that was how they drove donkeys in Platt German. God knows how those old drovers' calls originated.

Yes, the child, the 'little thing' . . . I reminded myself of how she was tormented and beaten, because of what was now imminent . . . As a boy, I had always suffered from a fear of thresholds, that wild fear of setting foot in a strange, completely unknown house. And when I finally went in, I was cowed and apprehensive, and naturally came a cropper. Animals smell fear. People smell fear. Things only improved when I learned that everybody has to die. But that took twenty years. The Platt German expresses the matter more pithily and with less pathos: 'What's he then? His bum's only got two halves!' Which is true.

And now I was a strange man going to a wicked, strange woman. I quickly played through the different scenarios of Hansel and the witch; 'but I'm so shy' . . . and then I recovered. It took much less time to happen than to write. It was over. A wise Indian said, 'You have to kill the tiger in your mind, before the hunt – the rest is a formality.' And Frau Adriani? I thought of my sergeant-major, and of the beaten, crying child . . . All right.

'Shut up!' the Princess shouted into a window where a parrot was squawking in his cage. 'Shut up! Or you'll be stuffed!'

The bird must have understood German, because it shut up.

Billie laughed. 'You wanted to buy some Worcestershire sauce as well,' she said, in one of those associations of ideas of which only women are capable.

'Oh, yes! Come on, we'll get it in Fructaffair, they've got everything.'

The Swedes spell some of their foreign words phonetically, which can be very funny. So we bought Worcestershire sauce. The Princess sniffed suspiciously at the stoppered bottle, and generally made the shop assistant's life as hard as she possibly could; Billie knocked over a jar of gherkins, which survived the experience and escaped with a shock, foaming briefly in their vinegar . . .

'Look, such a lot of salt!' I said.

The Princess looked at the barrel, 'As a child, I always believed that a single drop of water in a salt warehouse would consume the entire stock.'

That made me think so hard, I almost forgot to follow the other two, who were already standing in the street, nibbling raisins. 'We'll find a doll for the child,' said the Princess. 'Come along! Oh no, wait – I'll do it . . . no, Billie come with me!'

For a tiny instant, I felt sorry; I would have liked to stand on the pavement alone with Billie. What would we have said to each other? Nothing, of course.

'Did you?'

'We did,' shouted Billie.

'Let's see it,' I said.

'But not on the street!' she said.

'D'you think the dolly will catch cold?' said the Princess, and unwrapped the parcel. It was a Swedish girl, dressed in the national costume of Dalarne, bright and colourful. She was covered up again. 'For it is more blessed to wrap than to receive,' said the Princess, and tied the string. 'Well then, let's . . . Do you think she shoots, our dear lady?'

'Just leave her to me . . .!'

'No, I won't, Poppa. You only come into it if she becomes abusive, and the fur starts flying. You do the introduction, and tell her that we've got the letter and everything, and then I'll have it out with her.'

'What about me?' asked Billie.

'You lie down in the woods in the meantime, Billie, we can't possibly march up to the lady like an avenging army. Everything would be lost. Even two of us – it's this way – is too many. Two against one – the one will start growling before we've even said anything . . .'

'Well, you can hardly growl more than she does anyway. What a bitch!' I had taken Billie's arm.

'Are you managing to do any work here?' asked Billie.

'Not likely!' I said. 'I'm pausing for inspiration . . . you're a nice chap, Billie,' I said quite out of the blue.

'You young people,' said the Princess, and made a face like a well-meaning aunt arranging an engagement, 'I'm so glad you're fond of each other!'

I heard the undertone. At that moment I felt what real friends they were – there wasn't a trace of jealousy there; we three genuinely liked each other.

Now the path started to look familiar to me, there was the fence and there was the children's home.

Billie had walked slowly on, and we reached the door. No bell. They probably had no use for visitors here. We knocked.

After a long time, we heard footsteps approaching, and a maid opened the door.

'*Kan Ni tala tyska?*' I asked.

'Hello . . . yes, yes . . . what do you want?' she asked, smiling.

She was obviously pleased to be able to speak German with us.

'We'd like to see Frau Adriani,' I said.

'Yes . . . I don't know if she has time. Frau Adriani is just taking roll call, that is . . . she's inspecting the children's belongings. I'll just . . . one moment please . . .'

We stood in a grey, whitewashed hall, the windows were divided by wooden slats into little rectangles; like bars, I thought. A few portraits of Swedish monarchs hung on the wall. Someone came down the stairs. Her.

'Good afternoon,' we said.

'Good afternoon,' she said, quietly.

'We're here on behalf of Frau Collin in Zurich, and would like to talk to you about her daughter.'

'Do you have . . . a letter?' she asked suspiciously.

'Yes we do.'

'All right.'

She went on ahead and led us into a large room, a kind of hall, where the girls probably had their meals. There were long tables and an awful lot of chairs. In one corner stood a smaller table, where we sat down. We told her our names. She looked at us questioningly and coldly.

'Frau Collin asked us to keep an eye on her child — she is unfortunately not able to come to Sweden herself this summer, but would like someone to visit her from time to time.'

'I see to the child,' said Frau Adriani. 'Are you . . . acquainted with Frau Collin?'

'It would probably be best if we could speak directly with the little girl; her mother wants us to give her her regards, and there is a message to deliver.'

'What sort of message?'

'It concerns the little girl — of course I'll deliver it in your presence. May we speak to her?'

Frau Adriani stood up, shouted something in Swedish through the door, and came back.

'I find your behaviour more than a little strange, I must say. I find you conspiring with the child, intefering in my educational practices . . . What are you up to? Who are you anyway?'

'We have told you our names. By the way . . .'

'Frau Adriani,' said the Princess, 'no one wants to check up on you, or interfere with your work. You must take a lot of trouble over the children – I can tell. But we want to keep her mother informed of anything . . .'

'I can do that,' said Frau Adriani.

'Of course. We want to be able to tell her that we have seen her daughter happy and well . . . and how she's getting on . . . ah, here she is.'

Shyly the child approached the table at which we were sitting; she walked a little uncertainly, and stopped some way short of us. We looked at her; she looked at us.

'Well, Ada,' said the Princess, 'how are you?'

We heard Adriani's voice urge, 'Say hello now!' The child cringed, and stammered something like hello.

'How are you getting on?' Frau Adriani didn't take her eye off the child. She spoke as though from behind a wall.

'Fine . . . Thank you . . .'

'Your mother sends you her love,' said the Princess. 'She sends her love and then she asks you in this letter,' the Princess rummaged in her handbag, 'if Will's grave is being looked after? That must be your little brother?'

The child wanted to say yes, but she didn't manage it.

'The grave is well kept-up,' said Frau Adriani. 'I see to that. We visit the churchyard every fortnight, to do our duty. And the grave is well tended, I supervise that, I'm responsible.'

'That's fine . . .' said the Princess. 'And I've brought something along for you as well, a doll! There! And do you play nicely with the other girls?'

The child looked up anxiously and took the doll; her eyes darkened, she swallowed, swallowed again, then suddenly let her head drop and began to cry. It was heart-rending. Her crying transformed everything. Frau Adriani leapt up and took her by the hand.

'You'd better go back upstairs now . . . you've had enough of this! Your mother's sent you her love, and . . .'

'Just a minute!' I said, 'Ada, if you ever have something

important you want to tell your Mummy, remember, we're staying at Castle Gripsholm!'

'Nobody's telling anybody anything important here,' said Frau Adriani loudly, and went with the girl to the door. 'Come on you – get a move on! – what needs telling will be told by me – and just you remember that . . .' She carried on talking outside, we heard her scolding, but we couldn't make out any more of it.

'Shall I . . .'

'Don't row with her,' said the Princess, 'the child would only suffer as a result. We'll telephone Zurich, and then we'll see!' We got up.

Frau Adriani came back, very red in the face.

'Now let me tell you something,' she shouted. 'If you dare to show your faces round here again, I'll call the police! It's none of your business, you understand! It's outrageous! Get out of my house this instant! Don't ever darken my door again! And don't try snooping around here either – I'll . . . I'll have to get a dog,' she said, as though to herself. 'I'll write and tell Frau Collin what sort of people she's got herself – where's that letter anyway?'

I motioned to the Princess with my eyes, nobody answered, and we walked slowly towards the front door. I sensed the woman becoming ever so slightly unsure of herself.

'Where . . . where's that letter?'

We didn't speak, we didn't say goodbye, she had taken care of that already, we went out without saying anything. Threats? Making threats is a sign of weakness. We hadn't talked to Zurich yet.

When the woman saw that we were already at the front door, she started screeching uninhibitedly; we heard some hurried footsteps on the stone floor of the cellar below, the maids had assembled to listen.

'I forbid you . . . I forbid you to come here ever again! Get out of here! And don't you ever come back! Who are you anyway . . . two separate names! Why don't you get married!' she yelled at the top of her voice. And there we were outside. The door banged shut. Crash! There we stood.

'Hm!' I muttered. 'A great triumph.'

'Can't be helped, Poppa. She's just a bitch — what have we achieved?'

'We've got a pale No, as we say in Sweden. So we will telephone.'

'Just as soon as we got home. But if you don't tell Frau Collin properly what's going on here . . . the way the little mite looked! So fragile . . . and beaten! The way that woman kept on screaming at us . . . She's got steel hair. God, she deserves to be boiled in oil!'

I thought that was a bit wasteful.

We walked towards the wood where Billie would be waiting, and cursed Frau Adriani horribly. We looked for Billie. 'Billie! Billie!' No answer, not a trace.

'Do you suppose that red-haired devil is happy?'

'You do ask funny questions, Poppa! If *she's* happy . . .! The little girl's miserable! Damn it! What do we do? We help her! We can't stand around and watch! Damn it! Billie!'

We almost tripped over her.

She was behind a little mossy rise, in a hollow; she was lying on her front, with her long legs stretched out, knocking her feet together from time to time.

'Ah! Well, what did you say . . . what happened?'

We told her, both talking at the same time, and by now Frau Adriani had metamorphosed into a fire-spitting volcano, a veritable hell of devils, the head of a so-called school and quite simply a monster. Yes, she was a formidable woman.

I watched the two as they talked. How different they were! The Princess was deeply involved; the girl's sufferings had got to her, and her heart was shooting sparks. Billie felt sorry for the child, but she was like a stranger on the underground saying 'Sorry!' She pitied her in a decent, well-brought-up, quite impartial way. Perhaps because she hadn't witnessed it all as we had . . . The indifference of so many people comes from a lack of imagination.

'Let's go for a little walkas,' said the Princess.

'Where to?'

'Are you coming . . .? I'd like to see the grave. What a monster . . .'

The storm of outrage against the red-haired creature was slow to blow over. We went, making a wide detour round the children's home.

'When we get back – the very minute we do,' said the Princess, 'we'll book a call to Zurich. We've got to, *got to* get the girl out! Frau Adriani isn't without a certain charm!'

Billie was whistling quietly to herself. I stared at a dark group of trees, and read their leaves. I had wanted Billie; I felt I wouldn't get her, and now I had a moral reason for putting Lydia first. Billie didn't have a heart. It wasn't her heart you were in love with, you liar! Those long legs . . . Yes, but she's got no heart.

We walked slowly through the wood, the two had been chatting, and now they were *rabbling*. 'Rabbling' is a word for gossiping, running someone down. It was so fast, I was unable to follow it. Hopphopphopp . . . a pity we can't be around when other people are talking about us, because then we'd hear a more or less true opinion of ourselves. Because no one really believes it's possible to label people as briskly and unceremoniously as it's actually done. Or maybe one can label other people – but ourselves?

Billie was saying, ' . . . he promised her nothing, and when the time came . . .'

'More fool her,' said Lydia. 'Payment on receipt, my father alway said. Trust! Trust! There's only one sure way, and that's to use a man-trap. Don't you agree?'

Strange, I wonder where she got it from. Her own experience hadn't been that bitter . . .

Billie walked like a dancer: everything about her was graceful. She wore strange material – I didn't know the name of it, but it was colourful, coarsely woven stuff. Today, for instance, she looked like an Indian who had made herself a skirt from her wedding-tent . . . and so many bracelets! Any minute, I thought, and she'll throw her arms in the air, the beautiful savage, and, with a cry of love, plunge into the woods to join the others . . . A pity she doesn't have a heart.

'You see, there's the churchyard, over there! Yes, we'll get there before supper – come on!' We walked faster. A light wind had got up, then the gusts grew stronger, and a very soft rain started to fall. Sometimes the wind from the Baltic brought the smell of the sea with it.

We had reached the graveyard. There was a little wooden gate, and old trees towered over the low stone wall.

It was an old graveyard; you could tell by the weather-worn, somewhat dilapidated graves on one side. On the other side, however, the graves stood very tidily, in rank and file . . . well tended. It was very quiet; we were the only people to visit the dead this afternoon – to visit whom? You only go to the dead to visit yourself.

'Which row . . .? Wait a minute, she wrote it down in the letter. Eighteenth . . . no, fourteenth . . . one, two . . . four, five . . .' We looked for it.

'Here,' said Billie.

There was the grave. Such a small grave.

WILHELM COLLIN

BORN . . . DIED . . .

And a few wind-tossed flowers. We stood. No one spoke. Whether it was the scene earlier or the fact that it was such a tiny little grave, the contrast between the inscription 'Wilhelm Collin' and the little mound – it hadn't been a real Wilhelm at all, just a defenceless little bundle that should have been protected. There was one tear I couldn't stop, and it rolled down my cheek.

'Don't cry,' said the Princess, who was blinking. 'Don't cry! It's far too serious for crying!'

I felt ashamed in front of Billie, who was watching us sympathetically. Her eyes were warm. Quietly she said something to the Princess, and as they both looked across to me, I felt it must have been something friendly. I forgot that I had desired Billie, and took comfort from the Princess.

At Gripsholm, we booked a call to Zurich.

3

'It's a conflict between ethics and public morals, so to speak,' said the Princess, and we were still laughing as we sat down at the big table in our room. The lady of the castle had explained to Billie that it wasn't true that 'all Swedes always bathed naked', as one so often heard. Sometimes, of course, when they were bathing in tiny inlets, among friends . . . but on the whole, they were quite ordinary people, without any propensity for wildness, except that they liked spending money if there was someone else there to see it.

Outside, the rain fell in strings of pearls.

'What a happy rain,' said Billie.

And it was. It gurgled strongly, and up in the sky the brownblack clouds moved rapidly, or perhaps it was we who were so happy in spite of it all. It was good to be sitting in the dry and talking. What was Billie's perfume?

'What perfume is that, Billie?'

The Princess sniffed. 'One of her own concoctions,' she said. Was it my imagination – or did Billie blush a little?

'Yes,' she said, 'I brewed up something. I always mix up my own . . .' But she didn't say what it was called.

'Billie, can you help me? Have a look!' Since yesterday, the Princess had been working on a difficult crossword-puzzle. 'There's: Upland in Asia . . . Oh, I've got that one. But here: Oriental Man's Name . . . Wendriner? No, that can't be – Katzenellenbogen . . .? Nope . . . Fritzchen! Say something!'

'What is he really called?' asked Billie in indignation. 'Sometimes you call him Peter, and then it's Poppa, and now Fritzchen . . .!'

'His name's Kurt,' said the Princess, 'Coo-ert . . . That's not a name – if only he was called Ferdinand or Ulrich or something decent like that!'

Contempt all along the line. But now Billie's cultural selfesteem had been aroused: both heads bent over the newspaper. I sat by lazily and watched. And there, in front of the pair of them . . . Cock-a-doodle-doo – went a voice inside me, very quietly, Cock-a-doodle-doo . . . They whispered and curled up with laughter. I pulled at my new pipe, which was already partly broken in, and sat there with an expression that was meant to suggest good-humoured male superiority. Just then Billie said something which a reasonably wild imagination could interpret as very ambiguous, and the Princess sent a look darting in my direction: it was a tacit understanding among conspirators. Nocturnal conspirators . . . In the day time, we hardly ever spoke about the night – but there was some night time in the day, and some day time at night. 'Do you love me?' it says in the old stories. Only then – only then!

They gave up the crossword. 'We can try again after supper,' said Billie. 'By the way, do you fall asleep easily here? At home I usually have to read myself to sleep – but it's so easy here . . .'

'You should do it like Baroness Firks,' said the Princess. 'The Baroness came from Courland, of course, and the Courlanders are the apothecaries of Europe: they're all a little bit dotty. When the old lady couldn't get to sleep at night, she would sit on her rocking-horse and rock until . . . Yes? What is it?' A knock. A head poked round the door.

'Telephone? Zurich!' All three of us went.

A struggle for the telephone. 'Let me . . . can't you get off . . . for God's sake . . . Let me do it!'

Me. 'Hello!' Nothing. As always with long-distance calls, nothing at all to begin with. I heard a quiet buzzing in the earpiece. These noises vary, depending on which country you are calling; in France, for instance, there is a sweet, silvery trickling sound in the wires, and you become terribly nostalgic for Paris . . . Here it was buzzing. They had probably put in new copper wires to Switzerland, with all the political conferences . . . 'Mariefred? Please . . . !' And then quietly but clearly, a plaintive voice. Frau Collin.

'This is Frau Collin here. You wrote to me? How is Ada?'

'I don't want to alarm you – but you must be take her away.'
'Why? For God's . . .'

'No, the child's health is fine. But I'll write you a letter this evening, and tell you everything. This Frau Adriani is impossible. The child seems to be in terror . . .' And then I spoke out. I got everything off my chest, all my rage and pity, and my thirst for revenge after the defeat this afternoon and my loathing for domineering females . . . everything. And the Princess waved her fists in the air to encourage me. For a moment Frau Collin was silent.

'Hello?'

'Well, what should we do . . .?'

The Princess prodded me and whispered something. I shook my head: leave me alone.

'I suggest you write us a letter which will authorise us to take the girl away. And also send a cheque for whatever amount you may still be owing . . . if it turns out to be more, I'll be glad to make it up. And don't send it to the woman, because she wouldn't release the child straight away, but will go on torment-ing her instead – so write to us. Frau Adriani knows your handwriting. All right?'

An undecided pause. I gave a reference in Berlin.

'Well, if you think . . . Ah . . . but what will I do with the child then?'

'I've got some business in Switzerland – I can bring Ada to you, and we'll find somewhere else for her; but she can't stay here. Really – it's not on. All right?'

The voice complained, but sounded a little firmer. 'It's very nice of you to help me. You don't know me at all!'

'But I saw what was happening there . . . It really wasn't on. So you agree?'

'Yes. We'll do just as you say.' After a few further civilities we rang off. Done it. The other two did a wild dance right round the room. I held the receiver in my hand a moment longer.

'Thank God . . .' I said.

'Will she do it?' asked the Princess, still a little out of breath.

'What did she say?' asked Billie. Now she was slightly more involved; no longer politely sympathetic as she had been in the afternoon. Billie the trooper . . . I reported. Then all three of us danced.

'Terrific!' said Lydia. 'When will her letter arrive? Today's Tuesday. Wednesday . . . Thursday . . . In three days?' We all three shouted with happiness. I felt how sweet it is to do good, revenge paid back with interest, and love your neighbour as the hammer loves the anvil. 'Can I drive the young ladies to the pasture?'

We went to eat.

'Billie!' I said, 'if old Geheimrat Goethe could see you! Watering your wine! "Where did you pick up that revolting habit!" he said to the poet Grillparzer, when he saw him doing that. Or did he say it to someone else? But say it he did.'

'I hardly drink at all,' said Billie, and her voice sounded like a silver ring falling into a tumbler.

'More than Margot?' asked the Princess.

'Margot,' said Billie and laughed. 'I asked her once what she thought she would do if she ever got drunk. Because she never has yet. She said, I imagine being drunk would be like this – I'd lie under the table, with my hat on crooked, and I'd keep going miaow!'

We drank to that with a light red wine; Billie swallowed bravely, the Princess looked at me, tasted it and said, 'I don't really like red wine. But if the late Monsieur Bordeaux ever got to hear of it . . .' We talked about Zurich again and about the little creature, and Billie became animated, probably from watching us drinking. The Princess looked at her from the corner of her eye, well pleased.

I stifled a yawn. 'Are you sending everyone to bed, then?' asked the Princess.

'No, I'll write a letter to the woman first. You go on with your crossword!' They did. I wrote.

What was the matter with the typewriter tonight! Sometimes it has its little moods and the levers get caught up, the keys don't work, the ribbon sticks and I feel like thumping it with my first . . .

'Ha-hey!' called the Princess from next door. She was familiar with these developments, and I wrote on more quietly and a little ashamed of myself. There, it was done. Perhaps the letter was overweight . . . Haven't we got any scales?

'I'll take it to the post now!'

It was raining. I enjoy walking in a cool rain like that . . . How does the saying go? There's no such thing as bad weather, there are only good clothes. Well, there is such a thing as bad weather;

there is unsuccessful weather, empty weather, and sometimes no weather at all. The rain moistened my lips; I tasted it and took a deep breath: there's nothing to it, holidays, Sweden, the Princess and Billie – but it's one of the moments you'll remember later, and say to yourself: yes, you were happy then. I was, and I was grateful for it.

Back again.

'Well, did you solve it?' No, they were still working at it, and a bitter quarrel had just erupted between them. 'The father of church history' . . . they must have done something silly, because for this one clue they still had eight syllables left, among them e-di-son, who, although he had done much else in his life, and had transformed his time, surely hadn't fathered church history . . .

'Do that one later!' I said.

'When later?' asked Billie. 'We're sleeping later.'

'Billie's sleeping with me tonight anyway,' said the Princess. 'You can sleep next door in the ladies' boudoir.'

'Hurray!' the two shouted.

'Do you mind very much?' asked Billie.

'But . . .!'

She ran off to fetch her things, all those little bits and pieces every woman needs to keep her happy.

'She likes you, my son,' said the Princess. 'I know her. Isn't she a really nice person?' The Princess began to move things around and to arrange Billie's room. There was great excitement.

'What shall we do with the flowers?'

'Put them on the dressing-table!'

It wasn't an old Bordeaux – but it was a heavy Bordeaux. The little room was dimly lit from next door, it was so warm and secret, and we cuddled each other.

'Already?' I asked. The ladies wanted to go to sleep.

'But leave the door open when you're in bed – so I can hear what you're saying!' I went and undressed for bed. Then I knocked.

'Will you . . .!' said the Princess' voice. 'Disturbing honorable ladies at their toilette! Voyeur! Lothario! Bluebeard! What a race of idiots!'

But where was my eau de cologne? It was in there – that wasn't on either! Not for a gentleman. I gave another knock. Rustling. 'Yes?' I went in.

They were lying in bed. Billie was in mine: in loud pyjamas, with hundreds of flowers blossoming on them, she looked like the favorite wife of a Maharajah ... she was smiling coolly at her crossword. She was almost beautiful. 'What do you want?' asked the Princess.

'My eau ...'

'We used it all up!' she said. 'Now don't cry – I'll buy you some more tomorrow!'

I growled. 'Did you finish your crossword?'

'If we need you, we'll call you ... You can come and say good night to us!' I went over to them, and politely wished them both a good night, with two low bows.

'Billie, what a lovely perfume!' She said nothing; I knew what it was. The perfume was 'working' on her skin – it was not only the perfume, it was her. And she had chosen well for herself. The Princess got a kiss from me, a very slightly regretful kiss. Then I went. The door stayed open.

'Semi-precious stone,' I heard Billie saying. 'Semi-precious stone ... Let's see: sapphire ... no. Ruby ... no. Opal ... no. Lydia!'

'Topaz!' I called out from my room.

'Yes – topaz! What a clever boy you are!' said the Princess.

'No, no, don't you write it in – let me –' They were squabbling, the bedding rustled, paper scrunched ... 'Eeek –!' Billie squealed. Something tore.

'Silly noodle!' said the Princess. 'Right – now we'll copy it out again on this bit of paper ... Oh-oh, something's wrong! We crossed out some wrong syllables ...'

'Doctor Parchment solves puzzles without the aid of a pencil!' I called out. They weren't even listening. They were probably hard at work. Pause.

I heard the Princess, 'Puff ... Did you ever see anything like it? What's Puff?'

'Breath!' said Billie and I at the same time. It was like a secret understanding between us. They rustled some more.

'That's completely wrong! The essence of all sensory percep-
tion – sensory perception . . .' Now they were obviously at their
wits' ends, because they had both gone very quiet. I couldn't hear
anything.
'I don't know . . .' said the Princess. 'It's bound to be a
misprint!'
'You don't get misprints in crossword puzzles!' I called.
'You keep out of it, clever-dick!'
'Let me . . .'
'Give it here . . .'
'Do you have any idea?'
Both together: 'We don't know.'
'You need some adult assistance,' I said. 'Let me have a crack
at it.' And I got up and went in.
I took a chair and sat down near the Princess. For an instant,
the chair had hesitated in my hand; it had wanted to go to Billie's
side.
'Right – let's see then!' I read it, dropped the paper, picked it
up again, started again on a fresh piece of paper. They were
looking at me mockingly. 'Well?'
'It's not that easy!'
'He can't do it either!' said Billie.
'Let's have a go at the red wine first!' I said, and I did.
'That's very nice,' said the Princess. 'Wine-stains are every
housewife's favorite, particularly on sheets. What a pig!' She
was talking about me!
'You can wash them out,' I grumbled. 'Salt-stains are removed
by pouring red wine over them,' proclaimed the Princess. They
both lay on their tummies and pored over their newspaper. They
got nowhere. Billie had swept her hair back off her forehead and
looked like a baby. Like a picture of Billie as a baby. What a
round face she had.
'Ant . . . Antlers!' shouted Billie. 'Antlers for Hunting-
trophies! There, we hadn't got that one before! But where does
Chrys-chrys . . .'
'Me too!' Now I was half-lying on the bed with the Princess,
concentrating hard on the pencil-scribbles.
'Chrysoprase!' I said suddenly. 'Chrysoprase! Give it to me!'

There was an admiring silence from the two of them, and I basked in my cultivated vocabulary. We listened. A gust of wind rattled the window-panes, and the rain drummed in the night outside.

'It's cold . . .' I said.

'Come in with me!' said the Princess.

'You don't mind, do you, Billie?' Billie didn't. I lay very still beside the Princess.

'Character from Shakespeare's *Tempest* . . .' Gradually Lydia's warmth reached me. Something softly ran down my back. Billie was smoking and looking at the ceiling. I put my hand over – she took it and stroked me gently. Her ring flashed dimly. We were lying together like young animals – comfortably together, happy to be together: me in the middle, sheltered. Billie started to snarl.

'Why are you snarling?' asked Lydia.

'Just snarling,' said Billie. Character from Shakespeare's *Tempest* . . . Was it the word? The word tempest? When bees hear other bees buzzing angrily, they become angry themselves. Was it the word tempest? It started up in my shoulder-blades. I stretched very slightly, and the Princess looked at me. 'What's the matter?' No one spoke. Billie clicked my fingernails. We had dropped the newspaper. It was completely quiet.

'Give Billie a kiss!' said the Princess half-aloud. My diaphragm lifted – is that the seat of the soul? I propped myself up and kissed Billie. First of all, she just let me, then it was as though she was drinking me. Long, long . . . Then I kissed the Princess. That was like coming home from foreign lands.

Tempest.

It began as a light breeze – we were 'beside ourselves', because each of us was part of the others. It was a game, childish curiosity, delight at another's embrace . . . There were two of me, mirror images; three pairs of eyes saw. They flicked open the fan of womankind. And Billie was a different Billie. I was amazed.

Her features, her always slightly alien features, relaxed; her eyes were moist, tension disappeared and she reached out. Her pyjamas blossomed brightly. Nothing was planned, everything seemed natural – as though it was meant to be like that. And then we lost ourselves.

It was as though someone had been standing for a long time on the starting line with his bobsleigh, and suddenly the sleigh was released – it flew down towards the valley! We surrendered to the power which weighs man down and exalts him, to his lowest point and to his highest ... My mind was empty. Pleasure heightened pleasure, then the dream became clearer, and I sank into them, and they into me – we fled from the world's loneliness to each other. There was a grain of wickedness about it, a dash of irony, no romantic languishing, a lot of will, some experience and a great deal of innocence. We whispered; we spoke first about each other, then about what we were doing, then there were no more words. Not for a moment did the force that drove us to one another diminish. Not even for an instant did a crack appear. A strong sense of sweetness filled us, and now we were conscious, fully and completely conscious. I have forgotten a lot of things about this episode – but one is still with me today: that we loved each other most of all with our eyes.

'Turn the light off!' said Lydia. The lights went out, first the big chandelier on the ceiling, then the little bedside lamp.

We lay quite still. There was a faint glimmer at the window. Billie's heart was pounding, she breathed heavily, at my side the Princess didn't move. A scent rose up from the women's hair, and mixed with another, subtler one, perhaps the flowers or the perfume. Gently Billie's hand released mine.

'Go,' said the Princess almost inaudibly.

Then I stood next door in Billie's room, staring in front of me. Cock-a-doodle-doo – it went inside me, but soon stopped, and a strong feeling of tenderness wafted back towards them. I lay down.

Were they talking? I couldn't hear them. I got up again and crawled under the shower. A sweet tiredness came over me – and an almost irresistible urge to go to them and put roses ... but where can you get hold of roses at night ... what folly. Someone was at the door.

'You can say good night!' said the Princess. I went in.

Billie looked at me with a smile; it was a clean smile. The

Princess lay beside her, so quiet. I went up to each of them, and kissed them both softly on the lips. 'Good night . . .' and 'Good night . . .' The trees rustled loudly outside. For a second I stopped by the bed.

'How did all that come about so suddenly?' asked the Princess quietly.

Chapter Five

That was some throw! said Hans –
and he threw his wife out of the window

I

It was a day such as you usually get only at the end of summer: bright, heavy and windless. We lay on the shore by the lake.

A few yards away, a boat was bobbing around, our bathing-boat – the water gurgled quietly against the wood, up and down, up and down . . . If you put your hand in the water, you felt a tiny shock of cold, then you took it out again, and the droplets dried in the air. I sucked on a blade of grass. The Princess had her eyes closed.

'Today is the day before yesterday,' she said. That was how she calculated time, seeing as we were leaving the day after next, then today was the day before yesterday.

'Where do you suppose she is now?' I asked. The Princess looked at her watch. 'She's between Malmö and Trälleborg now,' she said, 'in an hour she'll be boarding the ferry.' Then we were silent again. Billie – I thought – Billie . . .

She had gone – quiet, happy, cheerful – and nothing had happened, nothing had happened. I was glad; it had cast no shadow. Thank God. I looked over to the Princess. She must have felt it; she opened her eyes.

'What's with Frau Collin? She's not natural. What sort of egg did she hatch from? The cat must have laid it!'

Frau Collin hadn't written – and we wanted to leave. We had to leave; our holiday was at an end. Telephone again? After all, in the end . . .

'Irritating woman,' I railed to myself. 'We've got to get the kid out of here! Bloody hell . . .'

'Poppa, you're an ambassador for your country!' said the Princess with dignity, as if the Swedish trees could hear us. 'You should remember your manners!' I used a word of one syllable. Whereupon the Princess splashed me with some Lake Maelar. I wanted to throw her in the lake. And found myself in it.

I snorted water at her like an elephant, she threw matches at me . . . then it all subsided. I crept back up, and we sat together peacefully once more.

'But what are we really going to do?' I asked dripping. 'Wait? We can't wait any longer! You have to be back on Tuesday, and they're lying in wait for me as well. A man has got to start working again some time! I'm just wasting valuable time here with you . . .'

She raised her arm threateningly. I moved away a little.

'I just thought. But shall we phone? Yes?'

'Let's first finish our swim,' said the Princess. 'And when we get back to Gripsholm, I'll tell you what we'll do. Now – hupp!' We swam.

'Listen,' I puffed, 'she won't do it, Frau Collin. She's probably had second thoughts about it – I got the impression she doesn't really want the little thing at home with her – maybe she has one of those wonderfully regulated lives . . .' The Princess pinched me in the leg. 'Or she doesn't trust us, and thinks we'll kidnap her daughter. But she trusted Frau Adriani. Well, you'll see! Women, really! But I'll tell you this, if she hasn't written today, I'll never do anything for other people's children again. Not for other people's! Not for yours! Not for mine! God!'

'Poppa,' said the Princess, 'for as long as I've known you, you've been holding forth about what you're going to do, and most of the time it turns out completely different. But men are like that. A bit deluded!'

'I'll . . .'

'Yes, you will. Take the future tense away from you, and you won't have much left.'

'Woman!'

'Same to you!'

Harrgh – and the whole lake started to pitch and toss, because we were having a furious sea-battle. We swam back to shore.

On the way back to the castle Lydia said, 'My boss hasn't

written at all . . . I wonder if they've sold him to a bordello in Abbazia?'

'Do you think there's any demand . . .'

'Cheri, have you seen the dachshund anywhere?'

'Your dachshund bag?'

'I thought he was under my bed. He barks at night.' We went inside.

The Princess whistled like a decoy bird. What was it?

The letter had arrived – a fat letter. She tore open the envelope, and I took it away from her. The pages fluttered to the ground. We picked them up and shouted for joy. There was everything we needed.

'That's marvellous! And now! What now?'

'The best thing would be,' said the Princess, 'to go straight there and get the girl out of those poisonous clutches. What are we waiting for?'

'Let's have lunch first, and then straight afterwards . . . A row is always good for the digestion.'

We were just eating our dessert of stewed cranberries when we heard a din outside the door that indicated something unusual was afoot. We dropped our spoons and listened. Well?

The lady of the castle came in; she looked like a special late edition.

'There is a child outside,' she said, and looked at us with a slight trace of suspicion, 'a little girl – she doesn't know your names, but she says she wants to go to the lady and gentleman who gave her a doll, and she cries all the time and is so red in her face . . . Do you know the child?'

We stood up at once. 'Oh yes – we know her all right.' We ran outside.

There was the little thing.

She looked as if she'd been dragged through a hedge backwards, she had been crying, her hair was all over her face, perhaps she had been running. She wasn't herself. When she saw Lydia, she ran quickly to her and buried her face in her dress.

'What is it? What's the matter?' The Princess bent down, and was transformed from the sportswoman of this morning to a mother; no, she was both. The lady of the castle stood there, brimming with curiosity – soaking it all up. Well?

The red-haired woman had beaten the child and smacked her and shouted at her so loudly, that the child had run away. She just hadn't been able to bear it any longer. The child was trembling violently and looking towards the door. Was she coming –? Frau Adriani was coming to get her! Frau Adriani was coming to get her! It was only piece by piece that we could find out from her what had happened. At last we had the whole story.

We stood around.

'I won't let her go back,' I said.

'No . . . of course not,' said the Princess.

'Will you not send the child back?' asked the lady of the castle.

The little thing started crying loudly: 'I don't want to go back! I want my Mummy!'

'Another black coffee,' I said to the Princess, 'and then we'll be off.'

We took the child back inside with us and piled biscuits up in front of her. She wouldn't take a single one. We drank our coffee quietly: when things are hectic, it helps to count up to a hundred or drink a cup of coffee.

'There, Lydia – now will you calm the child down and clean her up a bit while I telephone the old treasure. Would you please connect me with the children's home?' The castle-lady asked a lot of questions, I gave her some cursory answers, she said something Swedish over the telephone; I sat and waited.

Someone answered, in Swedish. I spoke German, on the off chance.

'Can I speak to Frau Adriani?' Long pause. Then a hard, yellow voice spoke,

'This is Frau Direktor Adriani!'

I introduced myself. And then she erupted.

'The child is with you then? Yes?'

'Yes.'

'You'll return her . . . You'll send her back to me immediately! I'll have her collected – no, you send her to me . . . You bring her back to me at once! I'll take you to court! For abduction! You put her up to it! You! What? If that child's not here in half an hour . . . in half an hour . . . Do you understand me?'

Inside me, a regulator snapped into operation, restraining the spring-action. I had myself fully under control. 'We'll be with you in half an hour!'

A click – she had hung up.

'Lydia,' I said, 'what now? I'll talk to the woman – it's her turn now. But the child's things . . . It's no good: we'll have to take her with us, or else we won't get all her belongings!'

'Hm!'

'And if we leave her here in Gripsholm, that woman's perfectly capable of coming here to snatch her, and the whole business will start all over again. Can you explain that to the little thing?'

It took ten long minutes. I heard the little one crying next door; she kept bursting into tears. At last she calmed down, and when the castle-lady spoke to her as well, she finally became quiet.

'Will you be sure to . . . will you be sure to take me back with you?' she kept asking.

We promised her, and set off.

So that the child wouldn't understand, we spoke in French.

'I hope you'll just throw the letter and the cheque in her face?'

'Lydia,' I said, 'I want her to rage for a while. Just a bit . . . I want to have another look at it all. Just for a little while!'

In disagreement, the Princess lapsed from French into her beloved Platt. 'You mean I'm to be savaged by a sheep, when I've got a dog in my pocket?' We turned back to the little one, who was becoming more uneasy with each step that took us nearer the children's home.

'Will I be able to get out again? But she won't let me – she won't let me!'

'We just have to collect your things. There's no need to be afraid . . .' When we saw the house, we fell silent. I quietly put my arm round the little one's shoulders.

'Come on – it'll be all right!' I had to pull her a little, but she came along quietly. We didn't have to knock – the door was open.

Frau Adriani was downstairs in the hall, bending over a chest with her back to us. As soon as she heard our footsteps, she spun round.

'Ah – there you are! Just as well for you! You didn't meet my maid, then? No? Well, there was someone coming for her, if you hadn't brought her yourself . . . Where did you run off to, you limb of Satan!' she screamed at the child. 'I'll be talking to you later! I've got something to say to you! Now get upstairs!' The child cowered behind the Princess.

'One moment,' I said, 'not so fast. Why did the child run away from you?'

'That's none of your business,' screamed Frau Adriani. 'None of your business! Come here, child!' She went up to the child, who shrank away in fear. She laid her hand on her head. 'What are you being so silly for? Why did you run away from me? Are you frightened of me? You mustn't be frightened of me! I only want the best for you! And you run away to strangers . . . can those strangers be closer to you than I am? I have explained to you, they're not even properly married . . .' She appealed to the child with false conviction, listening to herself; she spoke self-consciously, theatrically. 'Running away like that . . .!' The child shuddered.

'Could I possibly have a word with you?' I said gently.

'What . . . There's nothing to talk about!'

'Perhaps there is.' We all went into the dining-hall.

'So the child ran away to you! Wonderful! Just as well you returned her when I told you to! She won't be running away any more – I can promise you that. What a creature! She'll . . .'

'But the child must have had some reason for running away!' I said.

'No. Not at all. She had no reason.'

'Hm! And what will you do with her now?'

'I'll punish her,' said Frau Adriani, scenting blood and greedy for more. She stretched in her chair.

'May I ask you one question: How will you punish her?'

'I don't have to give you an answer – I don't have to. But I can assure you, because it's in accordance with Frau Collin's own wishes, with her own wishes, that the child receives a strict upbringing. So she'll be confined to her room, she'll be given some extra work to do in the household, she won't be allowed to go out with the others on walks – that's the way we operate here.'

'And if we were to ask you to remit her punishment . . . would you do that?'

'No. I couldn't agree to that. You could ask till . . . Was that what you wanted to ask?' she added sneeringly.

'But . . . do you treat all the children like that? Of course, one has to be strict some of the time, but to drive a child to the point of desperation . . .'

'Who's driving children to desperation! Bring up your own children! If you and this lady here should have any! And I'll bring up this one!'

'Go tell that to the marines!' muttered the Princess.

'What was that?' asked Frau Adriani.

'Nothing.'

'I have my principles. So long as a child is in my power . . .'

I looked her firmly in the eye . . . I let her wriggle a moment longer in her insane and impatient rage. Her eyes kept shifting from us to the child and back, she was waiting for the child. I thought about how many people like her held power over others. What would it be like if we really had to leave the child here; what did the other children have to go through . . .

'Right – now I'll make the necessary arrangements . . .' Frau Adriani stood up. Then I got to work.

'The child will not be staying with you,' I said.

'What?' she screamed, and put her hands on her hips.

'We're taking the child back to her mother. Here is a letter from Frau Collin, and here is a cheque. We'll pay right away!'

A wave of shock travelled across the woman's face like milk boiling over in a saucepan; you could see what she was thinking; you could hear her thinking, she didn't believe it.

'That's not true!'

'Yes, it's true. Now come along – sit down. I'll give you all the papers in turn.'

'You go upstairs!' she yelled at the child.

'The girl stays here,' I said. 'This is the letter. The signature is authenticated.' Frau Adriani grabbed it from me.

Then she threw it down at the Princess' feet. 'That's what I get!' she shouted. 'That's what I get for taking trouble over that neglected brat! That's my reward for caring for her! But you – *you* talked Frau Collin into it! You've set her against me! You've slandered me! I'll . . . Out! You . . .!'

'We're taking the child with us now. You will have her belongings packed immediately, and give me the bill. I will give you this cheque, drawn on a bank in Stockholm. And I shall need a receipt.'

Money! There was money at stake! The woman immediately cut to the new scene and her tone changed. Her new voice was much quieter, colder – and very firm.

'I'm unable to give you a bill at the moment. The child has broken a lot of things here, there are claims for damages. And of course, payment is due for a full quarter, that's the arrangement. Naturally. First I have to have an inventory made up, of all the things the girl has broken in this house. That will take at least a week to do.'

'You will write me out a receipt now for the amount of the cheque; it covers the costs up to the end of the quarter, with fifty-two Kroner over and above that . . . the exact sum you can settle with Frau Collin later. The child is coming with us.' The child had stopped crying, and darted constant looks from one of us to the other. She didn't let go of the Princess for a second, not a second.

Frau Adriani looked at the cheque, which I was holding in my hand. 'Money alone doesn't settle this affair!' she said. 'After all . . . Wait.' She went out. The Princess gave a nod of satisfaction. The woman came back.

'She's ruined a cupboard . . . she's broken a window; the window was bolted from inside, she must have thrown something at it . . . that makes . . . and I also have a laundry bill . . .'

'That will do,' I said. 'You will get nothing at all now, and we will take the child, even without her belongings – or else you give me a receipt for the cheque, and you let us have all the child's belongings' – Frau Adriani gesticulated – 'all her belongings, and you'll get your money. Well?'

She was wriggling; you could sense that she was squirming

and seething inside . . . but there was the cheque! Psychology can be very simple sometimes. No – not quite that simple. What a repertoire that woman had! Now she was down to her last record.

She started to cry. The Princess stared at her, as though at some fabled exotic animal.

Frau Adriani was crying. It sounded like someone blowing on a child's trumpet, a kind of squeaking noise, produced very quietly, and with completely dry eyes – like little rubber pigs when the air is squeezed out of them, and they crumple up, all wrinkled. 'I am a woman who has made a life for herself by hard work,' sang the toy trumpet. 'I have travelled a lot, and acquired culture. I have a sick husband; I have no one to help me. I have been in charge of this house for eight years – I am like a mother to the children, like a mother . . . the child is very dear to me . . . for this child . . . Little bleeders!' she screeched suddenly.

It felt like deliverance. The performance of the play, *The Compassionate Mother's Heart* had been so ridiculous – it was from the repertoire of a provincial hysteric – that it was like being released from a nightmare when she started swearing and came back to reality, to her reality.

'Now,' I said, 'now we can go and get packed!'

She flared up with one final moment of bravado, 'I'm not packing. You go up there yourselves, and collect her things. Probably all over the place anyway. I'm not going to look for them.' She threw herself into a chair, and immediately leaped up again. 'Of course I'm not letting you go up there by yourselves! Senta! Anna!' Two maids appeared. She said something to them in Swedish, which we didn't understand. We went upstairs.

Little heads were peering out of all the doors, frightened, curious, excited faces. No one spoke; one girl curtsied awkwardly, then others. We were up in Ada's dormitory; the four little girls who were in it huddled shyly in a corner. We opened the cupboard and the Princess asked about a suitcase. Yes, the child had brought one, but it was up in the loft.

'Would you please . . .' One of the maids went. The Princess cleared out the cupboard.

'This? And this one?' The door flew open, and Frau Adriani swept into the room.

'I want to see just what she's taking! I expect you'll probably pinch a few things while you're about it!' She was a bad loser – but who can remain decent when they've lost the contest?

'You can see everything for yourself, and besides – Hey!' She had made for the child, who ducked away. I stepped between them hastily. For a moment we looked at each other, Frau Adriani and I; there was enough physical intimacy in that look to make me shudder. This struggle was the obverse of love – like any struggle. And in those eyes I saw a deep chasm: this woman had never been satisfied, never. The old cynical prescription flashed through my brain:

Rp.
Penis normalis
dosim
Repetatur!

But that was not all. The atavistic drive of mankind was rampant in her: for power, power, power. Nothing hurts such a creature more than an unexpected rebellion. A world collapses. Spartacus . . . So many children were suffering here. I could have hit her. She shrank away.

The maid arrived with the suitcase; we packed in silence. Once the woman grabbed a little blouse and then threw it down again. The child held onto the Princess' hand. The little girls in the corner hardly dared to breathe. Frau Adriani looked over to them and jerked her head, they shuffled out of the door. The suitcase was shut. One of the maids wanted to help – Frau Adriani forbade it with a gesture. The suitcase wasn't heavy. The child followed quickly; she wasn't crying any more. Once I heard her take a deep breath.

'The receipt?' Frau Adriani went over to her desk, scribbled something on a piece of paper, and gave it to me, as though with a pair of firetongs. I very nearly felt sorry for her, but I knew how dangerous and how wasted such pity was. It wouldn't even have done her any good, because she would have used that emotional

honorarium to buy herself some new props, and the whole business would begin all over again. I gave her the cheque. I watched her face. The curtain was down – there was no more acting. The show was over.

Slowly we left the house where the little girl had suffered so much.

None of us looked back. The door closed behind us.

2

The last day . . .

I'm already dressed in my travelling-clothes, there is a remoteness between Lake Maelar and myself; we address each other formally.

The long hours where nothing happened; only the wind fanning my body, the long hours where I gazed at the sun shining. The long hours where I gazed at the water, the leaves hissed gently, and the lake splashed against the shore; empty hours in which energy, intellect, health and strength can be replenished from the reservoir of nothingness, from that mysterious store which will one day be empty. 'I'm afraid,' the storeman will say, 'we have nothing left . . .' And I suppose that's when I shall have to lie down.

There's Gripsholm. Why don't we stay here for good? We could take lodgings for a long period, sign a lease with the lady of the castle, it wouldn't even be that expensive, and then we would always have blue skies and grey skies, sun, sea-breath, fish and whisky – holidays forever.

No, it's not feasible. When you move, your worries follow you. If you're only staying somewhere for four weeks, you can laugh at everything – even the little unpleasantnesses. They don't concern you. If you stay there forever, though, you have to be involved. 'It's beautiful here,' Charles V said once to a prior whose monastery he was visiting. '*Transeuntibus!*' replied the prior. 'Beautiful? Yes, if you're passing through.'

Our last day. In all those weeks, we'd never had such a refreshing swim as this. The warm wind had never been so kind. The sun had never shone so brightly. Not as on this last day; last day of the holidays – last day of summer! A last sip of red wine, a

last day of love! Another day, another ship, another hour! Another half-hour . . .! When the taste is most delicious, it's time to stop.

'Today is today,' said the Princess — because now everything was ready for our departure: suitcases, handbags, dachshund, the little thing and us.

'You look a right mess!' Lydia said to me as we were going to say goodbye to the lady of the castle. 'You must have shaved with a cheese-grater! One really can't leave the boy on his own for a moment!'

I rubbed my chin ruefully, got out a mirror and hastily put it away again.

There was a lot of palaver with the castle-lady. '*Tack* . . . thank you . . .' and, 'Thank you very much! . . . *Tack so mycket* thank you . . .' and, 'All the best!' — a friendly and animated to-ing and fro-ing. And then we took little Ada by the hand, each of us picked up a bag, there was the little car . . . Away.

'Holiday *jok*,' I said. *Jok* is Turkish and means 'gone'.

'You really don't miss anything, do you,' said the Princess combing the child's hair.

'Lydia, I'd never have guessed you'd make such a good nanny! What great qualities you keep hidden away!'

'Just because I happen to be like an onion!' said the Princess, thereby disclosing, perhaps unwittingly, the essential nature of all her sex.

Slowly, very slowly and haltingly the child began to talk — we didn't force her to and at first she didn't want to at all, but gradually her tongue loosened. We saw how much she wanted to talk, how much she had to say, and she said it all:

The row over Lisa Wedigen; the leaf from the calendar; the constant punishments and the harebells under the pillow; her nickname 'the child'; little Will and Mummy; and all the things the Limb of Satan devised to tyrannise the little girls, and Hanne and Gertie and the food in the cupboard and everything.

It was a bit confused, and, although we understood the gist of it, from then on I called the little thing Ada Confusion. The Princess mothered and fathered the child at the same time. I suggested she should breastfeed the infant, and then there was a

fierce quarrel as to which breast: left or right. And so we reached Stockholm.

We were on our way back to Germany.

Berlin stretched out its giant arms across the sea . . .

'We'd better phone Frau Kremser,' said the Princess, 'just to be on the safe side. Boy, have we had a good holiday! And what do you want?' The girl had been fidgeting as if she had something to say, but then said nothing, 'Well?'

No, she didn't need the potty. She wanted to ask us something.

Which she did.

'Are you actually tramps?'

We looked at her, completely flabbergasted.

'Well, Frau Adriani said . . .' It turned out that Frau Adriani had represented us to the child as committed, yes, as professional tramps – 'those tramps out there, that aren't even married!' – and the child, by now completely thawed out, wanted to know; were we tramps, and where we'd tramped . . . and if we'd been married before, and why not any more, and then she did have to go to the potty, and then we put her to bed. I caught myself feeling a little jealous of the child. Who was the child around here? I was. But she fell asleep, and Lydia was once again all mine.

'Are you married?' asked the Princess. 'What a question!'

'Oh, woman,' I said. 'We're tramps, we can't be married. And if we were . . . Five weeks, that would be fine, Mhm! Without a cloud. No rows, no problems, no *histoires*. Five weeks aren't five years. Where are our troubles?'

We handed them in at the left-luggage office . . . you can do that,' said the Princess.

'For five weeks, yes,' I said. 'For five weeks, some things are fine, everything's fine.' Yes . . . intimate, but not bored; new, but not too new; fresh, but not too strange. Life went on, seemingly unchanged . . . The heat of the first few days was gone, and the long, lukewarm years were not upon us yet. Are we frightened of emotion? Sometimes of the form it takes. Anyone can manage to be happy for a brief time. A brief happiness: none other is conceivable, here on earth.

We rolled into Trälleborg. It was late in the evening; the white

arc-lights swayed in the wind and we watched as the carriage
was pushed onto the ferry. The child slept.

A large passenger-steamer swept through the water in the
harbour. All its lights sparkled: the ship's lanterns at the front,
little dots on top of the masts; every room, every cabin, was lit
up. There it went. Music drifted across.

Whatever you do –
my heart will still belong to you –

A wave of yearning swept our hearts. There went the illuminated happiness of others. And we knew that if we were sitting on
that liner and saw our own illuminated train on the ferry, then
we too would think, there goes happiness. Glittering and colourful, the great ship steamed past us, with the little dots of light on
its masts. We didn't see the sweating stewards, nor the ship-
owners in their offices, nor the quarrelsome captain and the
dyspeptic purser . . . of course, we knew they existed – but right
now, for this one moment, we wanted to forget.

Whatever you do –
my heart will still belong to you –

For a little while, our hearts sailed with them. Then our
carriage was on the ferry. The ship trembled slightly. The lights
on the coast grew smaller and smaller, then sank back into the
blue night air.

We stood on deck. The Princess drew in the salt breath of the
sea.

'Poppa, thank you for a lovely summer!'

'Oh no, girl, thank you!'

She looked across the dark sea. 'The sea . . .' she said quietly,
'the sea . . .' Behind us was Sweden. Sweden and a summer.

Later, we sat in a corner of the restaurant and ate and drank.

'To our holiday, girl!'

'And to what else?'

'To Karlchen!'

'Cheers!'

'To Billie!'

'Cheers!'

'To Adriani!'

'Boo!'

'To your Generalkonsul!'

'Half a cheer!'

'None of those are proper toasts, Poppa. Don't you know another one? You do know another one. Well?'

I knew what she was getting at.

'Martje Flor,' I said. 'Martje Flor!'

She was that Friesian peasant's daughter, during the Thirty Years' War, whom mercenaries dragged to the table; they had plundered everything, the wine-cellar and the smokehouse, the fruit-store and the linen-cupboard, and the peasant himself was standing by, wringing his hands. Roughly they had dragged the girl over – and there she stood, stubborn and not at all frightened. They wanted her to propose a toast! They flung a bottle at the peasant's face, and pressed a full glass into her hand.

Then Martje Flor raised her voice and her glass. There was silence in the room when she spoke her words, words which all Lower Germans know:

'Here's to long life and happiness!' she said.

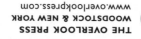

THE CASE OF SERGEANT GRISCHA by Arnold Zweig   1-58567-335-8

"The greatest novel on a war theme . . . from any country."   —J.B. PRIESTLEY

"Some experiences in literature are unforgettable and this is one novel that culminates in an overwhelming effect of power and protest and irony and pathos of human fate."
—The New York Times

THE SORROW OF BELGIUM by Hugo Claus   1-58567-238-6

"With biting wit, gorgeous language and graphic imagery, Hugo Claus rushes the reader back in time as if by magic . . . This immense autobiographical novel is clearly Claus' masterwork."   —DANIELLE ROTER, The Los Angeles Times

PAST CONTINUOUS by Yaakov Shabtai   1-58567-339-0

"I cannot recall having encountered a new work of fiction that has engaged me as sharply as Past Continuous, both for its brilliant, formal inventiveness and for its relentless, truth-seeking scrutiny of moral life."   —IRVING HOWE, The New York Review of Books

MOUNT ANALOGUE by René Daumal   1-58567-342-0

"A marvelous tale . . . as transparent and as inexhaustible as Pilgrim's Progress or a New Testament parable."   —ROGER SHATTUCK

"One of the most intriguing poetic reveries of contemporary literature."
—ROBERT MALLET, Le Figaro Littéraire

A NIGHT OF SERIOUS DRINKING by René Daumal   1-58567-399-4

"The book is Daumal at his witty, satirical, parabolic best. It demolishes all ordinary human concepts and then, in a final redemptive gesture, sends its protagonists out into the resulting chaos to 'pursue the business of living.'"   —P.L. TRAVERS

GREEN HENRY by Gottfried Keller   1-58567-427-3

"In no literary works of the nineteenth century do the lines of development that to this day determine our lives become so clear to us as in those of Gottfried Keller . . . His prose is unconditionally loyal to every living thing."   —W.G. SEBALD

THE MAN WHO CRIED I AM by John A. Williams   1-58567-580-6

"A forceful, penetrating story of commitment and disillusionment. . . . A powerful novel in which a dying Negro writer and intellectual tries to come to terms with himself and his country."   —ELIOT FREMONT-SMITH, The New York Times

Check our website for new titles

THE OVERLOOK PRESS
WOODSTOCK & NEW YORK
www.overlookpress.com